Collisi

Kristen Gr

Table of Contents

To Stacy, for showing me the kind of love
I wanted for myself, which in turn showed me the kind of love
I needed to create for my characters.

Chapter One: Cool as a Cucumber

I had barely walked through the door and I could already hear them whispering. I don't know why I was surprised; I knew they would be. It was so cliché: troubled girl walks through crowded cafeteria while everyone stops what they are doing to stare, leaning in and covering their mouths to mutter something to their friends. Part of me wondered what they were saying; the other part of me knew I was better off not knowing. Instantly, I had flashbacks to walking through the halls in sixth grade, right after everyone heard the news that my mother had up and left. That I could handle – this was worse. Focusing straight ahead, I tried to act natural, as if today was just like any other day; as if the past three weeks were just one awful nightmare that I would soon wake up from.

"Just breathe. Cool as a cucumber, remember?" The arm of my best friend linked with mine. Her words of encouragement only confirmed that I did not look natural at all.

"I do not feel very cucumber-like. This was a bad idea."

"Here. Sit." Shelly stopped next to an empty table and pulled out a chair for me. "What do you want – pizza or Chinese?"

"You are not going to leave me here alone with these vultures while you bring me a tray of food, like I'm some helpless cripple. I'm coming with you."

"How are you going to carry a tray of food with that?" She pointed to the sling cradling my left arm.

"Can we not, with the pointing?!"

"Yes, because it was my pointing that called attention to the big contraption wrapped around your arm."

I sighed as we made our way to the pizza counter. "Remind me why I let you talk me into coming here for lunch?"

"Because you needed to get out of the house... and because you were beginning to smell a bit ripe."

"The doctor told me I had to wait a few days before showering!"

"Two days. The doctor told you to wait two days. Not five."

I rolled my eyes and opened the refrigerator while Shelly ordered our slices. I tried to balance both of our soda bottles in one hand. It was difficult doing everything with one arm. It was even more difficult for me to ask for help.

"I'm serious," she continued, tucking her red hair behind her ear. "I don't think Febreeze is going to save that poor recliner you've been laid up in. We probably have to burn it."

I felt my cheeks push up as I tried to conceal a smile.

"There it is! There's the smile I was waiting for." She poked her finger into the dimple in my left cheek.

As I attempted to swat her hand away from my face, one of the soda bottles sprung loose from my grip and rolled across the floor. The cashier shot us a disapproving look. I quickly followed after the runaway bottle, and knelt down to catch it before it went any further. When I reached my hand out, a large-sized white sneaker stopped the bottle in its tracks. My eyes traveled upward – perfectly-fitting jeans, a white t-shirt that was tight in all the right places, broad shoulders – until they were looking into a pair of familiar eyes staring back at me. I quickly tried to stand when I saw who it was, but he bent down to help me up, and both of our heads knocked together. We recoiled, rubbing our heads in unison.

"You should be more careful crawling around on the floor with that arm," he said with a smirk.

"You should be more careful with that head."

"Are you okay?"

Ignoring his outstretched hand, I stood and brushed my pants off. "I'm good. I've been through worse."

His eyes tensed. "I know."

I immediately regretted my choice of words. I felt the tightening in my chest and averted my attention to the soda bottle still under his shoe. "Well, thanks for stopping that."

"No problem," he said as he picked it up. "Just don't try to open it any time soon, unless you're planning on wearing it."

"Don't worry. That one's hers." I pointed my thumb in Shelly's direction.

His smirk turned into a grin, revealing his set of impeccably straight teeth. "Here. You can carry things better like this." He stepped closer to me, and wedged the soda bottle into the crook of my elbow. The sling cradled it along with my arm and kept it from falling.

"Thanks." I quickly backed up and turned to make my way back to Shelly. I had only walked a few steps away when I heard his voice call from behind me.

"Merritt?"

I turned back around. His eyes were sincere and warm, a look I was not used to seeing on him. Then again, I had never actually looked directly into them.

"I'm sorry about your dad. I am glad you're okay, though."

I forced my best polite smile, one that I had rehearsed. "Thanks, Chase."

Shelly's eyes were wide with curiosity when I reached her back at the table. "What was that all about?"

I shrugged. "Nothing. He picked up the soda I dropped."

"Talking to Chase Brooks is never nothing. What did he say to you?"

I folded my pizza slice in half, and shoved a giant bite into my mouth. I smiled innocently as I chewed.

She shot me an annoyed look. "You will finish that pizza, and you will tell me what he said."

Chase Brooks had been the topic of conversation in town since his return several weeks ago. I did not mind, as it took the attention off of my tragic headlines. Shelly and I had known Chase since kindergarten. He grew up to be the quintessential popular kid who was good at everything. In high school, he started his own band with aspirations to become famous. After graduation, he left for California, and everyone thought he would make it big in the music industry. Two years later, he was back here in humdrum Staten Island, and working at his father's auto body shop. Nobody knew what happened in California, but it was clear that he did not end up rich and famous.

I took another bite of my pizza while I scanned the cafeteria. Chase was sitting at a table surrounded by his usual group of friends. From his messy-on-purpose blonde hair, to his thousand watt smile, he effortlessly looked the part of rock star heartthrob. Girls had always treated him as such, and he had always eaten it up. I knew early on that I wanted nothing to do with a guy like that – no matter how washboard his abs might be.

"He seems different." Shelly was looking in the same direction as I was.

"You haven't seen him since high school. Of course he looks different." I stuck my soda bottle in between my knees and tried to twist the cap off.

"Not physically. I can't quite put my finger on it."

"It's his eyes. They look sad."

"I wonder what happened to him." She shook her head. "Yet, the same girls are still trying to get with him."

"I just don't understand how girls like that are considered attractive."

"Their tits are pushed up into their throats. That's how."

"They leave nothing to the imagination. They're cows, giving all the metaphorical milk away for free. Are they that desperate for sex? There's so much more to life than two bodies converging for a physical release."

"I think a physical release with Chase is all those girls are looking for."

"Well then, they shouldn't act so surprised when he doesn't give them anything more after that." I grunted, still struggling with the bottle cap.

"I don't know why you insist on doing everything the hard way."

"I've almost got it."

"Tell me what he said to you before."

"I thanked him for picking up my soda. He said he was sorry to hear about what happened. We walked away. I told you – nothing major."

A smile began to spread across Shelly's face.

I rolled my eyes. "Don't start. That means nothing."

"That's not why I'm smiling," she said in a singsong voice.

Chase was standing beside my chair. He reached down and took the soda bottle out from between my knees. In one swift twist, he tossed the cap onto the table and handed the bottle back to me. He then pulled up a chair and sat.

"I was opening it."

"She means 'thank you'," Shelly quickly interjected.

He smiled. "I was just making sure the soda didn't explode all over you after you catapulted it into the air."

"Thanks. You're a hero." I took another bite of pizza.

"So, how long do you have to wear that for?" He motioned to my sling.

"Four weeks."

"She'll be taking it off at physical therapy this week, though," Shelly added. I tried to ignore the eyes she was giving me. I was not as thrilled as she was about Chase's presence at our table.

"If I actually make it to physical therapy."

A confused Chase looked to Shelly for an explanation.

"I have classes on the days they want her to go to physical therapy: Monday, Wednesday, and Friday. They don't have late hours, so I can't take her after class. Crazy pants over here thinks she's going to drive herself there with one arm."

"I don't see what the big deal is," I shrugged.

"You shouldn't take the risk," said Chase.

"Exactly what I said," agreed Shelly. "You don't need to be in another accident."

I cringed at the reminder.

"Why don't I take you?" Chase offered.

Shelly's eyes lit up.

"No way." I held my hand up. Don't be ridiculous."

"Why is it ridiculous?" she asked. "It's right by his dad's shop. It's perfect, actually."

"That doctor's office right across the street? I can take you there on my way in to work in the morning."

I shook my head. "No."

"Well, it's a good thing I don't ever take 'no' for an answer." Chase stood up and pushed his chair in. "Make her appointments for nine, Shell. I'll pick her up around a quarter-to."

"I can make my own appointments."

"Nine. Got it," Shelly replied.

"Hello! Does anybody hear me?"

Chase flashed his signature smile. "See you ladies Monday."

"Bye, Chase!" Shelly wiggled her fingers.

I blinked at my friend incredulously. "Are you kidding me?"

"What?" She shrugged, trying not to make eye contact with me. "You need a ride to physical therapy. Chase is going to take you. What's the problem?"

"The problem is that I don't want to be stuck with him for the next month. Who knows what he'll expect in return."

"He's not like that, Merritt."

"Whatever he is or isn't, I still don't want him to drive me around."

"It's better than you trying to drive yourself."

"I don't understand why. Most people only use one arm when they drive anyway."

"You can't drive with your arm in a sling. It's too dangerous and I won't let you!" She stood abruptly and stormed off to throw out her tray.

I was stunned by her outburst. I stood when I saw her making her way towards the exit, and had to take two steps just to match one of hers.

"Hey, giraffe legs, wait up!"

She did not slow down until she reached her car. She swung her car door open and got inside. I was out of breath as I plopped in beside her. "Well, at least I got my cardio in for the day."

Her expression did not change as she stared straight ahead, clenching the steering wheel in both hands.

I touched her shoulder when I realized she had tears in her eyes. "Hey, what's wrong? What the hell just happened?"

"These past few weeks have been hard for me, too, you know."

"I'm sorry. I know–"

"No, you don't know," she interrupted. "I sat in the hospital all by myself. They wouldn't let me see you because I wasn't family. I tried to explain that nobody else was coming but they wouldn't listen. I thought you were going to die. I replay that night in my head over and over again. I shouldn't have let you drive. If I had just talked to you a little longer, if I was able to get you to stop crying, if I had just taken your keys…" She trailed off as a tear slid down her cheek.

"Do not blame yourself. Please. The only person at fault was me. I was driving."

"I should have stopped you." She wiped her nose with the back of her hand. "But this time I'm going to stop you. You can't drive around with your arm in a sling. If Chase is offering to drive you, then you will let him."

I sat back in my seat. "That's what this is all about?"

"I can't lose you, Mer. This was a close call, and I never want to go through anything like it ever again."

I leaned over the center console and wrapped my good arm around her tightly. "You're not going to lose me. You know I'd just come back and haunt you forever."

"You can't make jokes like that now!"

"You've known me since we were five. You know I make jokes at inappropriate times. Don't act surprised."

She rolled her eyes as she turned the key in the ignition. "You need to do something about these defense mechanisms you have. You're never going to attract any good guys like that."

"I attract plenty of guys – with my sarcasm and morbid sense of humor. It's all part of my charm."

She finally broke a smile. "You did attract Chase today."

"See? Silver lining." I rolled my eyes.

As Shelly drove us to her apartment, I couldn't help but wonder why Chase was so eager to help me. It's not like we were friends – or even spoke to one another, for that matter. What did he think was in it for him?

Chapter Two: Day One

I woke up to the sound of dishes clanking together. It was one of the downfalls of having to sleep on the recliner in Shelly's living room. The pain in my back was another. I was thankful to have a place to stay after losing mine, and I was even more thankful to have a friend like Shelly to rely on. She was family. She was all I had left. Still, it was hard. I slowly tried to sit up without upsetting my shoulder. When my eyes finally came into focus, I froze.

"Morning, sunshine." Chase was sitting at the kitchen counter just a few feet in front of me, an amused expression on his face. He was dressed in his work clothes: grease-smudged jeans and a black short-sleeve button-down. His name was sewn onto a patch with red thread.

My hand rose up to touch the wild bun on top of my head, as I took my disheveled appearance into full account. I looked down at my favorite Cookie Monster pajamas, and cringed.

"Chase brought breakfast," Shelly offered apologetically.

"You didn't have to do that," I grumbled as I trudged over and slid onto a stool.

"That means 'Thank You' in Merritt speak," she explained.

"Nice pajamas. You look cute."

"Here I was, hoping my horrifying appearance would turn your stomach and cause you to flee in fear."

He grinned, which only infuriated me more.

Shelly placed a plate with a golden pancake in front of me. "Look. Your favorite."

I pushed the pancake around with my fork, trying to ignore her obvious stare. My mood was not going to change just because Chase Brooks had brought us pancakes. My dislike for him outweighed my love of breakfast foods.

"She's just nervous about today," she stated.

"I am not."

Chase shook his head. "Don't worry. They won't do much during the first week of physical therapy."

"How would you know?"

He rubbed his left shoulder. "I tore my rotator cuff in high school. I had the same sling you have on, and had to go to physical therapy for weeks after that."

"You tore it playing football." I remembered him walking the halls with an entourage of girls, clamoring to cater to his every need.

"It took me out for the rest of the season. I missed every game. I was so bummed that year."

I laughed.

Both Shelly and Chase looked at me wearing the same confused expressions.

"I was just thinking about how nice it would be if my problems were as minor as missing a few football games."

"I'm sorry," Chase started. "I didn't mean it like–"

"It's fine," I waved my hand and stood. "I'm going to get dressed so we can get this over with."

Part of me felt guilty as I made my way to Shelly's bedroom to change. It was nice of Chase to offer to drive me to physical therapy; it was also nice of him to come with breakfast. Shelly would tell me that I should not treat him so rudely. She was easily the nicest person I knew – the kind that made others strive to be like her. She was a fierce friend, and her abundant optimism made it nearly impossible not to be in a good mood whenever she was around. Unfortunately, one side-effect of her positivity was occasional delusion. She lived in a world where everything was sunshine and rainbows, and all people could be trusted. I did not understand why Chase would volunteer to help me out of the pure goodness of his heart. I was unsure of his motives, and when I felt unsure about someone – my guard remained up.

I brushed my teeth and lost yet another battle with my hair. Curly hair was difficult enough to manage with two arms, let alone one. Workout attire was all I could muster. After what I had been through, the last thing on my mind was what I looked like. It was hard to find something that I cared about now. Nothing mattered anymore.

When I returned to the living room, Chase stood with his keys in hand.

"Thanks for breakfast," Shelly said, prompting me with her eyes to do the same.

"Yeah, thanks. That was nice." I offered him a half smile.

"Maybe next time you'll eat a little more." He half-smiled back.

I opened the front door and waved to Shelly on my way out. We walked down the stairs to find Chase's black Plymouth Barracuda parked out front. I nodded my head in appreciation when we stopped at his car. "I forgot you drive a 'Cuda."

He raised his eyebrows. "You know what car this is?"

"What, because I'm a girl I can't know about cars?"

He said nothing as he swung open the passenger door for me. He jogged around the front of the car as I positioned myself inside and struggled with my seatbelt.

"Would you like me to help you?" he asked in an amused tone.

"No." Admittedly, I needed help putting my seatbelt on around the sling. I was in too much pain to maneuver around it, and blindly search for the interlocking buckle near my hip. He watched me for about thirty seconds more before he leaned across my lap to pull on the seatbelt and click it into place. His shirt smelled like fabric softener, as if it just came out of the dryer.

I watched him out of the corner of my eye as he backed out of the spot and began driving. I wondered if the kind of girls he dated knew what kind of classic they were riding in; I assumed not.

"You used to drive an old car, didn't you?" he asked after several minutes of silence.

"Oh, good. Small talk. Here I was worried this would be awkward."

He chuckled, seemingly unfazed by my sarcasm. "Was it a Camaro?"

"It was a 1970 Chevelle."

"Ah, yes. That was the car you were in when–"

"Yep."

"Look, I'm sure you don't want to rehash any of it, but if you ever want to talk about what happened, you can talk to me."

"I don't even want to think about it, let alone talk about it."

"Sometimes it helps to talk about it."

"It won't help." I kept my eyes fixed on the road ahead, and tried to relax.

"I'm sorry. I'd like to tell you it will get easier in time, but I don't actually know if it will. I think maybe you just get used to the pain."

I turned my head to look at him. "That's actually the most realistic thing anyone has said."

"People don't know what to say when someone goes through a hard time. It's not their fault. They just offer you objective words to make themselves feel less awkward talking about it."

"You wouldn't believe all the objective words I've heard. If I had a penny for every time someone has told me that I should feel lucky to be alive…" I rolled my eyes.

"So you're saying you don't feel lucky?"

"Let's see. My mother walked out without a second thought. My father was a mental mess for years after that, until he just couldn't bear the pain any longer and took his own life. Then, I wrapped my car around a tree and totaled the only piece of my dad I had left. I had to drop all of my classes because you can't attend school when you're in a two-week coma. I'm sleeping on my best friend's couch with the contents of my pathetic existence in boxes. My life is destroyed, and every morning I wake up wishing that whoever pulled me out of that car had just left me there to die. So, to answer your question, no – I don't feel very lucky."

It was silent inside the car after that. I did not mean to unleash my demons on him. I looked out the window and wondered how badly it would hurt if I jumped from the moving car, mortified over what I had admitted aloud. Like Shelly, and like anyone else, Chase would undoubtedly tell me it was wrong to think so negatively, and that it was not normal to wish I were dead. He would now look at me like I was a freak, if he hadn't already.

After what felt like an eternity, we pulled into a parking spot outside the doctor's office. I quickly reached for the handle on the door, but was pulled back by the seatbelt.

"You know, you have to unbuckle yourself before getting out of the car."

"I was just looking for the eject button." I slumped back into my seat, and waited for him to release me. When he didn't, I reluctantly raised my eyes to meet his gaze.

"Don't be embarrassed of your emotions. You don't have to hide them from me. How you feel is how you feel, and I totally get it. But you need to understand one thing: the people still here – the people that care about you – they feel lucky that you're alive. That's why they expect you to feel it, too."

Nobody had explained it like that. I thought about Shelly and all she had been through; throughout everything that happened to me, she was experiencing it right along with me. Wishing that I died was like a slap in the face to her. I could not see around my own misery.

He clicked the release button next to my hip. "Come by the shop when you're done and I'll take you home."

I nodded and hoisted myself out of his car without a word.

Chase's words resonated in my head for the entire hour at physical therapy, which helped take the focus off the pain in my shoulder. I actually did not mind the constant shoulder pain. Physical pain was easy to handle. People understand physical pain – they empathize with it. But when you are depressed, the only person they blame is you. They look at you with judging eyes, wondering why you can't simply snap out of it. As if it was a choice you were making on purpose, choosing to remain in mental anguish, and revel in it. My suffering was too intense for people to comprehend. No one could fathom stepping into my shoes. I couldn't blame them. Who would want to, even if they could?

I took my time as I walked over to Chase's family shop, letting the warmth of the sun beat down on my face. I didn't want to face him, or worse, the way he would look at me after getting a glimpse of the thoughts inside my head.

"Hi Merritt." Chase's mom was sitting behind the desk when I stepped inside. She greeted me with a warm smile as she stood up to give me a gentle hug.

"Hi Mrs. Brooks."

"Please," she waved her hand. "Call me Beverly."

Beverly was tall and slender with blonde hair, the same color as Chase's, settling around her shoulders. She wore minimal makeup, but she did not need it. She had natural beauty. Her kind personality had always shone right through her face. Growing up, I often wondered what it was like to have a mother like her.

"Chase is in the back," she said, motioning to follow her through the door to the garage.

I inhaled the familiar smell of motor oil and rubber as we walked through the doorway. I looked around at all the heavy machinery and tools everywhere. My eyes rested on a pair of legs sticking out from underneath a Honda. They rolled out when we walked over to reveal that they belonged to Chase's father. I would have known whose father it was anywhere, just by looking in his eyes. Chase may have his mother's hair color, but he looked exactly like his father.

"Hi, Merritt." Tim wiped his hand on a towel hanging from his belt loop. He reached his hand out to touch my arm. "How are ya hanging in there, kid?"

"I'm hanging."

"Good, good."

"Busted axle?" I pointed to the vehicle he had rolled out from under.

Tim's smile spread from ear to ear. "Snapped clean in half."

"They must have hit a pretty bad bump."

"Kids these days wear their cars down to the bone until something breaks."

"Chase, come save this poor girl from your father's shop talk," Beverly called.

"I don't mind, really," I reassured.

Chase finally emerged from the far corner of the garage. His hair was now smashed under a backwards baseball hat. His trademark grin spread across his face as he approached me.

"How was it? Not too bad, right?"

"They could barely get my arm to move, so we're taking it slow."

"Chase cried like a baby the first day of physical therapy!" Tim exclaimed.

Chase's eyes widened. "I did not!"

"Alright, Tim. Back to work," Beverly chuckled as she playfully pushed her husband. Tim wrapped his arms around her to give her a lingering kiss before she disappeared into the front office. They were sweet.

Chase waited until they were out of earshot. "Look, Merritt. I'm sorry I made you upset before. I just–"

I held my hand up to stop him. "It's okay. I already forgot about it."

He hesitated a moment, and then nodded.

"I love the way it smells in here."

"You do?"

"It's that kind of scent that reminds you of your childhood. It takes you back to a certain memory whenever you smell it."

"Like old library books."

"The ones with the yellowed plastic around the covers," I agreed. Looking around, my eyes settled on a car covered by a tarp. "What's under there?"

"Just a car that was dropped off for some body work." He turned to face me. "Why don't we grab lunch before I take you home?"

"No, thanks. I'm not really hungry."

"You didn't eat breakfast this morning."

I shrugged. "I don't have much of an appetite."

"That's not what I remember."

"What's that supposed to mean?"

He smirked. "You were never one of those girls who just ate a salad."

"How would you know what I ate?"

"Shelly's birthday party senior year, I watched you inhale two cheeseburgers and a hot dog in less than five minutes. It was impressive."

I hoped my burning cheeks weren't as red as they felt. I wondered why he remembered anything about my eating habits. "I was just hungry that day."

"You need to eat so your shoulder can heal."

"And you need to get back to work. Let's go."

"Fine. But next time, we're getting lunch."

"Fine."

Chase held up his pinky.

I rolled my eyes. He held it out more prominently, until I had no other choice but to interlock my pinky with his.

I waved goodbye to his parents before we stepped out into the parking lot.

"So… how do you like living with Shelly?" Chase asked as he roared his engine to a start. "I know you guys have been best friends for a long time."

I shrugged. "It's fine, I guess."

"You guess?"

"I just feel bad. She and Brody were talking about moving in together right before everything happened. He's been dying to move out of his parents' house. Now their lives are on hold because of me."

"It's not because of you. Your friend is helping you until you can get back on your feet again. That's what friends do."

"I know. But that doesn't make me feel any less guilty."

"I'm guessing you weren't able to keep your house after your dad passed?"

"Nope. He owed too much, and I wasn't able to make the payments. Once my shoulder heals up, I'll be able to work and save up as much as I can to get my own apartment. I've been trying to find something to do to make money in the meantime, but haven't had much luck. There's not much I can do with one arm."

"You're still pretty banged up," he said, gently. "You should take this time to rest. You can worry about everything else later."

"Easy for you to say."

"I know, I'm not in your shoes. But everything has a way of working itself out. You can only focus on the here and now… and right now you've got to heal."

It would be comforting to believe that everything worked itself out; it certainly was a nice notion.

"You know, we have a small space on the side of my house. It's above the garage. I know my parents were looking to rent it out, but then everything was put on hold. It's vacant."

"They should put an ad online. Lots of people search for apartments that way. You can post pictures, too."

"I'm telling you about it, in case you wanted to get out of Shelly's place."

"Oh, no. I couldn't do that. I don't have money for rent. I don't even have furniture to put in an apartment."

"It's already furnished. My parents moved my old bedroom set in there when I moved to California. There's a refrigerator in there that we use to store extra food around the holidays, and a small kitchen with a sink and stove. It would be perfect for you."

I shook my head. "That's kind of you, really. But I still wouldn't have money for rent."

I could see the wheels still spinning in his head as he unclicked my seatbelt when we pulled up to Shelly's place. "Okay. I'll see you Wednesday. Don't forget we're going to lunch after."

"How could I forget? We pinky promised."

He grinned. "Are you ever not sarcastic?"

"Sure. When I'm asleep." I smiled as I swung the car door shut.

Chapter Three: Lunch Date

As pinky promised, Chase took me to lunch after physical therapy on Wednesday. We sat across from each other at the diner, looking over our menus while I hummed along to the song playing in the background.

Chase shot me a suspicious glance.

"What?" I asked defensively.

"You like Journey?"

"Who doesn't like Journey?"

"Touché."

"Nobody can belt it out like Perry."

"That's only because you haven't heard me sing yet."

I raised an eyebrow. "How do you know I haven't?"

"You never came to any of my shows."

"Your shows were in your garage. It's not like I was invited."

"You wouldn't have come if I did."

"Touché."

"I just didn't peg you for a rock chick."

"Well, there's your first mistake: trying to peg me as anything." I stared back at my menu, pretending not to notice Chase's deliberate stare from across the table. It was strange being around him; I had known him my whole life, but I did not truly know him. We were practically strangers, yet he did not feel like one.

"What?" I asked again without looking up from my menu.

"You look nice today."

I laughed looking down at my tank top and yoga pants. "I wasn't trying to."

"You really don't have to."

"I'm sure anything looks good after seeing me in my Cookie Monster pajamas."

"Are you kidding? You looked adorable."

His sudden compliments aroused nothing more than my suspicions. I put my menu down and leaned toward the table. "Let's get something straight here."

"Okay." He had an amused expression on his face as he crossed his arms over his broad chest.

"Your charm is not going to work on me. I don't care that you're in a band, or that you have a smile straight out of a toothpaste commercial, and I am not going to sleep with you. I don't know what you're trying to do here, but it won't work. Got it?"

His head tilted back as he laughed. "You think I'm doing this just to sleep with you? Why would you think that?"

"Let's see." I placed my finger on my chin pretending to think. "There's Jen, Kelly, Colleen, and Sarah for starters. Shall I name your other conquests?"

His eyes widened. "Conquests? I've never slept with those girls! Except for Colleen, but we were dating for a while back then."

I held up my hands. "Hey, you don't have to explain yourself to me."

"Don't I, though? You're accusing me of sleeping with girls I've never actually slept with."

"There's obviously a reason why people have that impression."

"I don't give a shit about what people think."

"So then why bother explaining yourself to me?"

"Because I care about what you think."

I rolled my eyes. "Spare me the you're different speech."

The waitress appeared at our table, and I was grateful for the interruption.

"What are we having?" she asked impatiently, without even looking up from her pad.

"Cheeseburger, well-done, with sweet potato fries," I said.

"Same for me," Chase replied. "Regular fries are fine."

"You got it." She walked away just as quickly as she came, and it was just the two of us again.

One corner of Chase's mouth slowly turned up. "A toothpaste commercial, huh?"

I rolled my eyes, but wished those words had not slipped out. "You have nice teeth is all I'm saying."

"What else do you think about me?"

"I think it's nice that your whole family works together at the shop."

"It is. You know my brother, Tanner?"

"I've seen him around." Everybody knew Tanner. The Brooks brothers looked nothing alike, but girls swooned in the same slutty manner over Tanner's tall-dark-and-handsome appearance. Chase was the oldest of three siblings. He and Tanner were two years apart; their younger sister, Khloe, was four-years old – and clearly unplanned.

He took out his phone to show me the background wallpaper on his screen. "This is Khloe."

Leaning over, I saw a picture of him and Khloe in a pool. She was exceptionally cute, smiling ear to ear in her two-piece striped bathing suit. She had his eyes that lit up when they smiled.

"She's adorable. She looks a lot like you."

"So, you're saying you think I'm adorable?"

I rolled my eyes. "Not what I meant."

"You know, one day you're going to roll those beautiful brown eyes right out of your head."

"And I'm sure it'll be because I'm with you."

He grinned proudly.

"Your parents seem so happy together. Like they're still in love. It's sweet."

His expression changed as he picked up a sugar packet and began to fiddle with it in his hands. "Yeah. They're great."

I had clearly hit a touchy subject. I remained quiet when the food arrived, unsure of what I had said to upset him.

"How come you haven't asked me why I'm back from California?" he asked, without looking up from his plate.

"I figured you would bring it up if you wanted to talk about it. It's none of my business."

"You would just sit there and wonder, and never ask?"

"I know what it's like when people ask questions about personal things. If you want to share it with me, then you will."

This was the first time I had seen him look less than his usual confident self. It was interesting to watch, like a magician about to reveal the secret to his trick. He ran his fingers through his hair, and continued to play with the sugar packet.

"I want to share it with you."

"Okay."

"Before I tell you, you have to promise that you won't say anything about this to anyone."

I groaned. "Are we going to pinky promise again?"

"Not even Shelly," he pressed.

"You do know how best friends work, right?"

"I'm being serious, Merritt."

"I'm sorry. Your sudden detour down Serious Lane caught me off guard." I held my right hand up to make my vow. "I won't tell a soul. Not even Shelly."

He finally put down the sugar. "When I got to Cali, I bartended. It was the quickest way to make decent money. There were always people scouting the local bands that would play there. I handed my demos out to anyone that would take them."

"Did you get any call backs?"

"The owner of the bar actually turned out to be friends with a talent agent. He said he knew of a band that was in need of a singer. We all met up, and we just clicked. We would practice at the bar on nights when I wasn't working. We sounded really good." His eyes sparkled as he reminisced about California life.

"It sounds like it was going really well." I could not understand why he chose small town life working at the family auto repair garage over making his dreams come to fruition.

"I had to come home, though. It's my dad." He finally looked up at me. "He's sick."

I put down my burger. "Sick?"

"My mom called one night with the news. It's cancer… colon cancer."

My heart sank. "Oh, Chase. I'm… I'm so sorry."

"I was afraid to tell you. I didn't want to upset you."

"Your dad has cancer, and you're worried about upsetting me?"

"You just lost your dad. I didn't want this to trigger you."

I was quiet for a moment, letting it all sink in. "How bad is it?"

"The cancer hasn't responded to the treatments. It's not looking good. The doctor said he won't make it past… he won't make it to next summer."

I wanted to reach across the table for his hand, but my hand remained in my lap, unable to move. "I think it was really selfless of you to leave everything behind and come back home to take care of everything. You're a good son."

Chase smiled a smile that I recognized all too well – the kind of expression people make when they are smiling through the pain. The mouth puts on a show, but the eyes give it all away. His usual spirited eyes looked so sad just then. That was the difference Shelly had noticed days before. It hit me that I was not the only one sitting there in pain.

He would need strength and support in order to endure the coming months with his father's illness. It now made sense why he had a sudden interest in talking to me; he knew I had experienced loss and grief, and wanted advice from someone who experienced it firsthand. I was not too sure I was the right person for the job. I could barely get up most mornings, let alone provide strength and comfort for someone else; then again, maybe we could pull each other through it all, somehow.

"Now I get why you always change the subject. Think you could use your powers of diversion for me, too?"

"I can definitely do that." I held out my pinky. "I need you to make me a promise, right here and now."

He raised his pinky to mine, a curious expression on his face.

"You need to promise me that you won't hold anything back, or keep anything from me, just because you think it might make me sad. I don't need anyone to protect my feelings. I'm a big girl – I can take it."

He locked his pinky around mine. "I promise."

I squeezed his pinky before letting it go. "I mean it. If I find out you're not telling me something, I'm going to be mad… and you won't like me when I'm mad."

"Will you turn big and green?"

"Maybe."

"Do all of your clothes get shredded off, too?"

"Not the point. You should be very afraid."

"Speaking of the Hulk, that new Marvel movie coming out next week looks good."

"I haven't seen the trailer."

"How could you not have? Have you been living under a rock?"

"I've been kind of busy lately. You know, coma and all."

"Oh. Right," he said sheepishly. "Well, maybe we can go see the movie when it comes out."

My first instinct was to say no, but I caught myself before I shook my head. Shelly would never be interested in a movie like that, and I did love superhero movies. "Sure."

"Great."

We chewed in silence. It seemed to be our thing. We would talk until we were quiet, and then we'd let the quiet be. We were content, without the need for typical conversation filler. When the waitress came by to drop the check off, Chase stopped her with cash already in his hand before she could even place the bill on the table.

"Wait!" I scrambled for my wallet so that I could give her my portion, but she had already walked away. "How much was it? Here, I have a ten. Is that enough?"

Chase was laughing when I looked up. "I got it. Let's go."

"No, no. You are taking my money. I don't need you to pay for me."

"Put your money away. Let's go, or I'm leaving your handicapped ass here."

I gave him my best scowl as I put my money back into my wallet and scooted out of the booth.

"That look was actually intimidating," he teased as we entered the parking lot. "I felt a little scared there for a second."

"Good. Remember that look."

When we approached his car, he intercepted the door handle to open it for me.

"I do have another arm, you know," I reminded him, waving my good arm around. "You don't have to keep opening doors for me."

"I'm not opening the door for you because your arm is in a sling. Has nobody ever done this for you before?"

I said nothing as I eased myself into the seat. I was not about to get into my past love life.

He reached in and fastened my seatbelt.

"This just makes me feel like a child," I admitted.

He paused after he heard the click, his face inches from mine. "It's ok to need help sometimes."

"It just makes me feel pathetic, not being able to do stuff on my own."

"You're not pathetic at all. You don't always have to do everything on your own. You have people you can lean on."

"I know."

"Not just Shelly. You have me, now. You can lean on me."

I allowed myself to hold his gaze. Looking into his eyes was like watching a horror scene: even though you know you should look away, to save yourself the heartache, you can't seem to peel your eyes from it no matter what you do. He seemed so sincere. I wanted to believe him – to trust him – but I knew better.

He closed my door and walked around to the driver's side. My head fell back onto the headrest and I exhaled the breath I had been holding. I concentrated on the car in front of us as we made our way back to Shelly's.

"So, I spoke to my mom about having you stay in our apartment. She said she wouldn't charge you rent. Gas and electric would be covered, too."

I turned in the seat to face him. "You asked your mom?!"

"Yeah. She was totally fine with it. She said the space was going to waste just sitting there, empty."

"I already told you: I don't have money for rent, and I am not living there without paying. I can't believe you'd even ask her. She probably thinks I'm some loser moocher, or something!"

He laughed, which only fueled my fire. "She does not think you are a loser, or a moocher. She knows what you're going through. She knew your dad, and said she would be honored to help his daughter in any way that she can."

"Awesome. More pity offers. Now she'll think I'm ungrateful if I don't say yes. I can't believe you!"

"I'm sorry. I didn't think you were going to be mad about this. I'm just trying to help you out."

"I don't need your help, Chase. If I needed it, I'd ask for it."

"See, I don't think you would. That's your problem. You don't ask for help. You'd rather just struggle and suffer alone."

"That's my choice to make. Not yours."

"You said you felt bad about staying in Shelly's apartment. I found a space for you. What's the big deal?"

"I can't stay in your parents' apartment for free!"

The car slowed to a stop as Chase put the car in park in front of the apartment.

"We've known each other our whole lives. My mom knows you're going to take care of the place. She's happy to do it."

"We haven't known each other at all… and you didn't even ask me. You put me in such a weird position now."

"I was just trying –"

"To help, I know. Everyone wants to help, but they can't." I pushed through the pain and managed to unfasten my own seatbelt. I left the car as quickly as I could, and up the stairs even quicker. Shelly was still at school, so I paced in the silence. My phone sounded, undoubtedly a text from Chase. I switched it to silent and tossed it onto the chair.

I recognized that my anger did not come solely from Chase, but I certainly threw it all at him. I was furious that I was even in this position to begin with – homeless – without a place to feel comfortable and to call my own. It was a painful reminder of the home I once had. I knew none of this was Chase's fault, but it wasn't mine either. That was what angered me most of all. I was mad at the world for the hand I was dealt. It wasn't fair. I tried everything I could to make things better, but things only got worse. So what was the point in even trying?

Chapter Four: Prince Charming

"Help!" I screamed, as loud as I could in between coughs. The flames were surrounding me now, and it was almost impossible to breathe. I tried to cover my face with my hands, but only one of them lifted up. It felt like my other arm was crushed against something; I strained my eyes to see, but black smoke filled the car. I attempted to scream for help again, but inhaling just made me cough harder. It was unbearably hot. I was sweating so much it felt like I was melting. I wiped my forehead with my hand, and I realized it wasn't sweat that was streaming down my face – it was blood. I was stuck, and there was no way out. I closed my eyes. Panic turned to terror as I let the truth sink in: I was going to die.

When I opened my eyes again, I was no longer in the smoke-filled car. I blinked a few times, trying to allow my brain to register where I was. It was dark. My chest felt damp under my tank top. I was sweating. I reached up to wipe my tear-stained cheeks. Finally, I was able to focus on neon green numbers on the cable box. I was in Shelly's living room.

"Jesus, Merritt. That was worse than the last one."

I jumped hearing Shelly's voice right next to me.

I heard her sigh, but could not see the expression she was wearing on her face. "You had another nightmare. I heard you screaming like usual, but it was harder to wake you up this time."

I relaxed back onto the recliner, trying to catch my breath. "I'm sorry. Go back to bed."

"Was it the same, again?"

"Yep. Always is."

"I really wish you would talk to someone. It might help."

"Go back to bed. I'm sorry for waking you."

She sighed again, and walked back down the hallway.

I glanced back at the cable box. Shelly had about three more hours until she had to be up for class. I felt beyond awful for waking her up each night, but I could not escape the terrors in my dreams.

Every time I drifted off to sleep, the events from the night of my accident flashed through my mind like a scene from a movie: the streaming blood, the sound of glass shattering, and the smell of the fire engulfing me. Unlike reality, though, the person who pulled me out of my burning, mangled car that night never comes. So whenever I fall asleep, I end up being burned alive.

For the next few hours, I kept myself up reading one of Shelly's love story novels. I secretly loved a good love story. I was a bitter sceptic trapped inside a hopeless romantic's body – it was my curse. I knew it was ridiculous; there was no way these characters existed in real life. That's why people wrote about them, after all. Love stories are like religion; people need something to believe in, something to cling to, even if they never actually find out whether it exists.

At eight, Shelly pranced past me into the kitchen. Her wet hair was wrapped in a towel as she poured a bowl of cereal and perched herself on top of the counter. "So…?"

"So, what?"

"So, how was lunch with Chase yesterday?"

"It was lunch."

She dramatically slumped forward. "Merritt, please. I'm in a long-term relationship. I salivate at the thought of a first date with a guy. Work with me here!"

"It was not a date. It was lunch."

"Just give me details!"

"Shit, okay." I covered my ear. "Anything to stop the whining!"

She smiled triumphantly. "What was he wearing?"

"Dude, he was in work clothes. I told you, this wasn't a date."

"Does he get all covered in grease smudges at work? Does he wipe sweat from his forehead with the back of his hand?" She acted it out dramatically.

"Yes, come to think of it, there was an eighty's montage, too. He ripped off his shirt and started dancing all about the garage. It was very Kevin Bacon."

She shot me her usual disapproving look, but continued on. "What did you talk about?"

"We talked about music, about his family – that Khloe is so cute."

"She is. The whole Brooks family just has an awesome gene pool."

I nodded in agreement. "Then I called him out on all the girls he sleeps with."

Her eyes widened. "Mer, you did not! What did you say?"

"I let him know that I was not interested in being one of his groupies. He claims he doesn't have sex with them."

"Well, if you're not going to have sex with him, what does it matter who else does?"

"It doesn't. Just own it if you're doing it."

"What did he say when you said you weren't interested in him like that?"

"He laughed!"

"He probably didn't know what to do with himself." Shelly puffed out her chest and deepened her voice. "You're not interested in me? But I'm Chase Brooks. Everyone is interested in me."

I giggled. "It wasn't like that. He's actually not as full of himself as I thought."

She raised her eyebrows. "So you had a good time with him?"

I shrugged. "It was okay."

"I don't know. Chase offering to be your personal chauffer, and taking you to lunch is still pretty major. I think he's got a crush on you."

I rolled my eyes. "Highly doubtful. I'm one cup size and several hundred brain cells shy of being his type."

"I think it's time you started dating."

"And I think it's time you took your meds."

"You haven't been out on a date in a really long time – that's just not healthy!"

"I'm touched at your concern for my health."

"You've been through a lot. Don't you think it's time to try to get back to normal? You can't really enjoy life when you're missing out on such a huge part of it."

"Just drop it, okay?" I could not remember what normal even felt like anymore.

"I'm your best friend. I'm not allowed to drop it." She crossed her arms over her chest. "Just go on a date, have some fun. No big deal. You have to come out of your comfort zone once in a while."

"But I like my comfort zone. It's comfy here."

"Just because your mom left you doesn't mean you can't trust anyone else ever again. Don't let her win."

"You know, everyone out there has daddy issues. Sure, they might have low self-esteem… maybe they become strippers… but they're all walking around having pretty normal lives. When you have mommy issues, though, that shit runs deep. You must be pretty screwed up if your own mother can't love you."

"She didn't leave because she didn't love you. The mother who abandons her child is the one who is screwed up. Not the child. I bet she thinks about you every single day."

"I hope she doesn't think about me. Ever. If she regretted her decision, it would make everything that much worse. I hope she found whatever it was that she was looking for, so at least it was all worth it in the end." I glanced at the clock on the stove. "You'd better go get ready. Class starts in twenty."

"I wish you were coming with me."

I sighed. "I do, too."

I walked back to the recliner and turned on the television. Having to drop all of my classes this semester due to my extenuating circumstances not only set my graduation date back, but it was yet another thing that alienated me from campus life. Shelly and I were having the average college experience, and we were always together. Now, her experience continued while mine was on hold.

Ten minutes later, Shelly swung her bag onto her shoulder and grabbed her keys off the breakfast nook. "I'll see you tonight."

"It's Thursday – aren't you staying at Brody's?"

"Not tonight. Maybe Saturday… or whenever."

"Why?"

"I don't know. I told Brody I wanted to stay home with you tonight."

"Shelly, I'm fine. You haven't seen much of Brody lately, and I don't need any help around here. My other extremities work just fine. Seriously, go bang your boyfriend."

She bit her bottom lip while she contemplated it. "Are you sure you don't mind?"

I pointed to her room. "Go pack your bag."

She quickly disappeared into her room, and I could hear the sound of her toiletries being tossed into her duffle bag. Just because I had to sit home every night didn't mean she had to.

When she emerged from her room once again, she kissed the top of my head on her way to the door. "Love you, Toad."

"Love you, Frog."

My eyelids felt heavy from lack of sleep, but I was too afraid to close my eyes. The hours passed slowly as I tried to keep myself occupied. Two movies, a long shower, and four-hundred pages later, I heard my stomach growling. It was a little after six o'clock, but I ignored it; the fridge was empty with the exception of milk and jelly, and I had no interest in walking anywhere.

The sound of my phone startled me. It was Chase. I had not responded to any of his phone calls or texts since I left him in the parking lot yesterday. I was trying to figure out what to say before he picked me up for therapy in the morning, but nothing had come to me. If I didn't answer now, though, I'd have to deal with the awkward conversation in person.

"Hello?"

"Hey, open up before I drop something."

"Open up?"

"Yes. Your door: the big rectangular thing that lets people in and out of the apartment."

I rolled my eyes as I got up from the chair.

Chase was carefully balancing two fountain drinks on top of two take-out containers as he walked up the stairs when I opened the door. "You know, I could actually hear you rolling your eyes at me on the other side of the phone."

"What is all this?"

"This is dinner." He walked past me and set everything down on the kitchen table. Then he began rummaging through the cabinets. "I saw Shelly on my way out of class, and she mentioned you'd be by yourself tonight. I hope you like tacos."

"She mentioned I'd be by myself, or she told you to check up on me?"

"She mentioned it. I figured you needed dinner." He stopped to face me. "I know you don't want my help. If you want me to leave, I can go."

I don't know if it was the look on his face, or the hunger speaking. "Well, I can't let perfectly good tacos go to waste."

He smiled.

We sat down and let the crunching of tacos fill the silence. I was grateful I decided to shower today. I was also grateful to not be in pajamas with a Muppet on them. Chase sat across from me in a white t-shirt and black basketball shorts. I noted how his sleeves fit snugly around his biceps, and then silently scolded myself for noticing.

"So, how long were you planning on ignoring my calls?"

"I didn't have a specific timeframe."

"Well, if you would have answered sooner, you would have heard me tell you that I am sorry for talking to my mom about the apartment. You clearly told me you were not interested, and I kept pushing the issue."

"Don't worry about it. You don't have to be sorry."

"But I am."

I shrugged and kept crunching on my taco.

"You're not into apologies, are you?"

"Nope. Why apologize for something that you meant to say or do? People are only sorry because they don't want the other person to continue to be upset. It's like when someone kisses a wound; it doesn't actually make it feel better – it's just something people do."

"Or people are truly sorry for what they did because they didn't realize how much it would upset someone… and we kiss wounds because that's how we show we care. You're very cynical for someone our age, you know."

"I'm told it's one of my redeeming qualities."

"You have many."

"Sure. If you're into people with avoidant personality disorder."

He laughed and shook his head, taking another bite of his taco. His square jaw tensed as he chewed.

More crunching in silence. I knew it was my turn. I swallowed my bite, and then I had to swallow my pride.

"I didn't mean to freak out over it. You were trying to do something nice, and I overreacted. I appreciate you asking your mom about the apartment. I've been thinking a lot about it, actually."

"You have?"

"I can't keep staying at Shelly's. She's got her own life, and I don't want to interfere."

"Something tells me she doesn't look at it that way."

"She doesn't. She'd never say so, but I know she is tired of being woken up in the middle of the night, and she feels like she can't have Brody over. I feel like I'm putting her entire life on hold."

"What's waking her up in the middle of the night?"

I looked down at my lap, wishing I hadn't let that part out. "I just have nightmares sometimes."

"Sometimes?"

"Every time I try to sleep, I have this recurring nightmare. It's terrifying, so I guess I scream in my sleep... and it wakes her up."

Chase's eyebrows pushed together. "What is happening in your dream?"

I wanted to say I didn't remember, but he was watching me too closely. He'd know I was lying, and call me out on it. "Do you know any of the details about my accident?"

"Just that you were pulled from your car after you crashed into a tree."

"Well, the dream is very vivid. It's like reliving that night over and over. I can feel the blood gushing out of my head; I can smell the burning from the fire. I wait to be rescued, but it never happens... so I'm trapped."

"How does it end?"

"I close my eyes and accept the fact that I'm about to die. That's usually the part when Shelly wakes me up."

His eyes looked far away. I knew he must have been searching for the right thing to say.

"Hopefully your parents put some really good insulation in that apartment, so I don't wake up the entire household."

His eyes raised up to meet mine. "Are you saying you're going to take it?"

"I'd like to talk to your parents first."

"You can tomorrow, after therapy."

I nodded.

"Speaking of tomorrow, you should come out to Big Nose Kate's tomorrow night."

I scrunched my nose. "I try to avoid crowds with this contraption."

"I bet you could get a lot of free drinks with a sling."

"I don't need a sling to get free drinks."

"Touché. Shawn is throwing himself a birthday party at Lucky's. Brody is going. I'm sure he'll want to bring Shelly. It'll be fun." He kept his eyes on me while I mulled it over in my head. "I mean, I'll be there. What more could you ask for?"

"I'll think about it."

"What's to think about? Just come."

"Something tells me you'll show up here anyway, whether I say yes or not."

He grinned. "Now you're getting it."

I really was not getting it at all. Since he started driving me to therapy, I had eaten breakfast, lunch, and dinner with Chase; now he wanted to hang out on a Friday night? None of it made sense.

He stood and tossed our containers into the trash can. "I'm in the mood to watch a movie. Got any good ones?"

I raised my eyebrows. "You're staying?"

"Do you have somewhere else to be?"

"I just might."

"Who's the lucky guy?"

"I don't think you know him. He's tall; rides a horse. He'll be here at nine to whisk me away in his shiny armor."

"Prince Charming? I'm right here!"

I smirked as I stood to bring my plate to the sink. Chase quickly followed and grabbed the sponge.

"If you're a prince, where's your horse? I don't see one outside."

"Oh, it's there - all four-hundred and twenty five of them." He grinned, proud of the horsepower in the hemi engine parked out front.

I laughed as I shook my head.

"You should do that more often."

"Do what?"

"Laugh."

"I laugh when things are funny."

"You don't laugh enough around me."

I shrugged. "I guess you're just not that funny then."

"I'm funny!" He flicked water from his fingers onto my face.

I paused for a moment, contemplating my counterattack. I reached into the sink and scooped out a handful of soap suds at him in retaliation.

He keeled over at the waist, holding his right eye. "Ow! It burns!"

"Shit! I didn't mean to–"

Before I could finish my sentence, he had the sink hose in his hand, pointed at me like a squirt gun. He squeezed the trigger, and I squealed as the spray of cold water hit me. This meant war. I snatched my empty cup out of the sink, and began filling it with water.

"Okay! Truce!" Chase held up both hands, dropping the hose into the sink.

I acted like I was putting the cup back into the sink, but spun around on my toes to dump the water over the top of his head. He tried to get away but his foot slipped in the puddle of water now on the floor. His feet went up, and he fell down onto the tile.

I burst into laughter.

Chase was laughing, too, as he ran his fingers through his wet hair. "You're lucky your arm is in that sling!"

I was doubled over, and could barely catch my breath. "If this is how you're going to make me laugh, you can fall on your ass every time we're together."

"And you said I wasn't funny."

I couldn't remember the last time I laughed that hard. I ripped off a few paper towels and knelt down to dry the floor beside him.

"So, Prince Charming, huh? That's who you're waiting for?"

"I'm not waiting for anybody. Life's not a fairy tale. Princes don't come along on their white horses and rescue women from their terrible lives."

"Tell that to Cinderella."

"Please. Cinderella loses a shoe and it leads her perfect guy right to her. In real life, if a girl loses her shoe at midnight it just means she's drunk."

"You can't fool me, you know. You wear that tough cynical skin on the outside, but I don't believe it for one minute. I know who you really are."

"How could you possibly know me? You've never said two words to me before last week."

"Just because we've never spoken to one another doesn't mean I don't know what kind of person you are."

"And what kind of person do you think I am?"

"I didn't say I think I know who you are. I said I know you. I know you have a huge, caring heart that you protect behind the stone wall you put up around it. You always stuck up for the kids who were being bullied in elementary school, even though they were bigger and stronger than you. I know you are super smart, and always did well in school. I know you and Shelly would chase butterflies on the playground every day during recess. I know you dated guys that you were too good for. I know you took care of your father when your mom left. I know she hurt you. I could see it in your eyes. I know you were different after that. I never knew her, but I hated her for changing you. I also know your dad was your world, and I know how much you miss him."

I sat on the floor of the tiny kitchen, stunned. All this time I had known him, never once did I think he gave me more than a passing glance.

"What happened?" he asked carefully. "What happened to that girl?"

"A lot happened. My father wasn't the same after my mother disappeared. Something inside his brain snapped, as if he had no idea how to continue on without her. At thirteen, I had to pick up the pieces of our broken lives. I spent all of my time with him, when I wasn't in school, trying my best to cheer him up and take care of the house. The man who never had more than a beer or two on occasion began finishing bottles of vodka by the day. His drinking became such a problem that his job eventually let him go. I babysat after school to earn as much quick cash as I could, returning home by seven to cook dinner for someone who was already passed out for the night. I ate alone, cleaned alone, and paid the bills alone. I did everything alone because I didn't have any other option. When all I wanted was someone to help me, help never came."

"So you learned early on that the only person you could depend on in life was yourself."

"Sometimes, you're all you've got in this world."

"You don't have to be alone anymore. You have me, for what it's worth."

I looked into his eyes. The striking shade of dark green was illuminated by the light brown sunburst around his pupils. "Why didn't you ever talk to me? Why watch me from a distance and not say anything?"

"Honestly, I didn't have the guts."

"So, what changed?"

"Everything. Coming back from California to find you like this. My dad, your dad. Do you believe things happen for a reason?"

"I don't know what to believe anymore. It's hard to think there's a reason this all happened to me, like there's some stupid lesson I'm supposed to learn from it."

"Well, I believe it. Whatever the reason is, I don't think things happen by coincidence."

"It almost seems like life is one big domino set. I crashed my car because I was drunk; I was drunk because I was depressed after having to bury my father; my father killed himself because my mother left us…" I trailed off.

"So, what do you think set off the domino effect? Why do you think your mother ran off to begin with?"

"That has been the million dollar question I ask myself every single day. Part of me feels like the reason could never be good enough to justify it; the other part of me feels like I would feel better if I knew what the hell happened. I never got closure." I shook my head. "It's always the people who you are closest to that hurt you. And they're the ones you can't let go of."

"Sometimes in life, you have to give yourself closure. Let it go. You'll drive yourself crazy otherwise. If she moved on and doesn't care, sad as that is, then you should forget her, too."

I felt a smile creep onto my face. "Give yourself closure. I like that."

"See? I'm not so bad to talk to after all."

I looked down at my lap, sheepishly. "I should have never judged you as harshly as I did."

He shrugged. "It happens. Just promise that you'll get to know me. The real me. Not the version you conjure up in that head of yours."

I held out my pinky. "I promise."

Chase smiled his wide grin, and locked his pinky with mine.

Chapter Five: Big Nose Kates

"Gimme a sec!" I shouted over the incessant banging coming from the other side of the door.

"Come on, Merritt! Just let me see!" Shelly whined.

Glancing at the time on my watch, I continued to fuss with my chest in the black tank top I had chosen to wear.

"This sling is way too tight," I said as I swung open the door. "Can you adjust it for me?"

Shelly's eyes lit up, staring directly at my overly pushed up C cups. "Holy boobs! You look hot!"

I rolled my eyes and turned back to the mirror. "They only look this big because they're being squished together by this stupid thing. Loosen the back a little?"

"I think you should leave it exactly the way it is."

"I really don't feel like pulling an Elizabeth Swan in the middle of the bar tonight."

"Why not? I bet Chase would cut you out of it." Shelly wiggled her eyebrows.

I shot her a look.

"Fine! You never let me have any fun." She loosened the strap much less than I wanted, and I knew that was all I was getting out of her.

"Chase is more Will Turner than Jack Sparrow, by the way."

The doorbell, followed by Shelly's high-pitched squeal, signaled that Brody and Chase had arrived. I had a knot in my stomach all day, and it only twisted tighter as I got ready to leave. Shelly would never let me out of going tonight. I took a deep breath as I surveyed myself in the mirror one last time before shutting the light.

"Doesn't she look hot?" Shelly asked as we entered the living room.

"Stop." I jabbed her in her ribs while I watched Chase's eyes survey my exposed legs in the short denim shorts I had chosen to wear. The humidity during summers in New York caused my hair to expand five inches all the way around my head, so I had to draw the attention elsewhere.

Brody laughed as he gave me a hug. "Merritt, I miss your face! I was happy to hear you would be coming with us tonight."

I had known Brody since he moved next door to me in third grade. He and Shelly liked each other much more than friends from the instant I introduced them. He was the Cory to her Topanga, and I couldn't have picked a more perfect match for my best friend. He balanced out her fiery personality with his levelheadedness, and he was fiercely loyal. Everyone who knew him loved him, and he was the only student to successfully befriend people from each social circle at Tottenville High School.

"You don't come around anymore." I made an obvious glare at Shelly.

He smiled and hung his arm around Shelly's shoulder. The scrawny dark-haired boy with freckles and missing teeth had turned into a tall and toned man with piercing blue eyes. "We didn't want to be a bother to you. You needed your rest. How about I make you ladies breakfast in the morning?"

"Your pancakes should make up for the empty space you left in my heart."

"She doesn't smile at me like that when I bring her pancakes." Chase nudged Brody with his elbow.

Brody laughed. "Breakfast foods are the way to Miss Adams' heart."

"And chocolate chip cookies. Oh, and rock music," Shelly chimed in.

Chase pretended to write a note on his hand. "Breakfast, cookies, music. Got it."

I shook my head and swung open the front door. "You are all idiots."

"You really do look great," Chase whispered as we walked outside to his car.

"So do you." His jeans and polo combination, that would have looked average on anyone else, seemed to be tailored to fit his exact measurements. The yellow shirt brought out every facet of color in his hazel eyes.

"Wow. A compliment?" He clutched his heart. "I will cherish it forever."

I rolled my eyes, but could feel myself smiling as Shelly and I slid into the back seat. Maybe the night would not be as bad as my nerves were anticipating.

As we pulled up to the bar, I stared out the window at the rundown, wooden shack that was Big Nose Kate's. Horseshoes were stamped into the cement stairs leading up to the door, and a tall bush was trimmed into the shape of a cactus outside. The Old-West-style saloon seemed out of place in the northern city we lived in, but the food was delicious so nobody really questioned it. Friday nights especially attracted a huge crowd with a local band playing all the typical cover songs from the eighties and nineties. There was already a line to get in, and it was only nine o'clock.

Brody's friend, Nick, was checking IDs at the door. He did a double-take when he saw me walk up alongside Shelly.

"Hey, Adams! Look at you!"

"Put your eyes back in your head, Nicky." Shelly patted his shoulder as he let us in ahead of the line.

"Hey, Nick." I followed quickly behind Shelly. I did not feel like getting into conversations with the people I had not seen since the funeral.

Inside, the wooden floor creaked under our wedges as we made our way to the bar. The musty air mixed with smells of sweat, cologne, and desperation of girls that were trying way too hard. A band was setting up on the small stage near the tall windows. I noticed several pairs of eyes on me as we walked over to our friends at the bar. I wondered if it was because of my accident, or the fact that I was walking alongside a Brooks brother. I tried my best to ignore the stares.

Kenzie and Tina were waiting at the bar for us. Their eyes were wide as they looked me up and down. Their mouths fell open when they saw Chase walk up beside me.

"Doesn't she look hot?" Shelly yelled over the blaring music.

"Would you stop saying that?" I hit Shelly's arm, a little harder this time.

"Nice rack, Adams!" Tina joked, poking my cleavage with her index finger. "Where have you been hiding these puppies?"

I shot her a look and swatted her hand away. She was worse than Shelly.

"You look great," Kenzie laughed, squeezing my arm. "I'm so glad you came out tonight. We've missed you!"

"I missed you, too."

Tina and Kenzie were sisters, but they could not be more different. Tina's dark bob suited her tough, punkish exterior, her skin was covered in colorful tattoos. Kenzie looked like a blonde-hair-blue-eyed southern belle; she was the younger, and sweeter, of the two. We had been friends since freshman year of college. They lived on the other side of the island. Though the island was small, people that lived on the north shore rarely came to the south shore, and vice versa. Each end of the island had everything one would need, so there wasn't a reason to leave. Tonight, the sisters had ventured down to the south end of Staten Island to see me.

Shelly turned to Chase, motioning to the girls with her thumb. "Do you know Kenzie and Tina?"

"Hello, ladies." Chase gave them a wave.

"You guys are packing this place out tonight. How do you feel?" Tina asked him.

"I can't wait. It's been a while. Hopefully I don't sound like shit."

I scrunched my nose up in confusion. "What?"

"Oh, I didn't tell you?" He grinned. "I'm the band that's playing tonight."

"No, you somehow forgot to mention that."

"Well, if you'll all excuse me. I have to go set up."

"Break a leg!" Kenzie called.

Out of the corner of my eye, I watched him head to the stage. I wondered why he had not told me. If he was worried about how he would perform, he certainly did not show it. He shook hands, or whatever that thing is that guys do, with all of his bandmates, who I now recognized very well. They were the same guys he played with in high school, only with less acne and slightly better style. They hadn't played since Chase left for California, and the bar was filled with anticipation, and little standing room.

"Earth to Merritt." Tina waved her hand in front of my face. "I know he's gorgeous, but try not to be too obvious."

I rolled my eyes. "Move your purse so I can sit."

Kenzie looked at me. "What is going on there?"

"Nothing," I replied quickly. "There is nothing going on."

"I keep telling her: Chase Brooks hanging around is not nothing," Shelly stated. She already had four small glasses lined up in front of her, filled with a bright pink liquid. She picked the first one up and tried handing it to me.

"No way," I protested.

"Come on, just one!"

I shook my head. "Just be happy I came out tonight."

"Fine, but we're toasting you anyway!" She wrapped her arm around me. "To my best friend in the whole wide world, who came out tonight even though she didn't want to!"

The girls threw their heads back and let the cool liquid slide down their throats.

"Enough of this girly shit. Let's get some whiskey!" Tina leaned over the bar and flagged down the bartender.

"How are you feeling?" Kenzie asked. "You don't always answer my texts, and I don't know if you even feel like talking about anything."

"I'm sorry if you feel like I've been ignoring you. I'm just having a hard time with everything. Everybody keeps asking how I'm doing – but how many times can I say the same thing, you know?"

Her eyes were filled with worry. "We came to visit you every day, in the hospital. Shelly told you, right?"

I squeezed her hand. "She told me. I appreciate your support. I really do."

"Did you ever find out who pulled you from your car?" Tina asked.

"No. Nobody came forward."

"That's a shame. Why wouldn't the person want recognition for such a heroic deed?"

"And the hospital gave you no details?" I knew Kenzie was trying not to pry, but everyone had the same question on their minds.

"Nope," Shelly shook her head. "They said the emergency staff took her in such a hurry because of the shape she was in, nobody paid attention to who the person was."

"It was just a good Samaritan. If he or she doesn't want to be found, then I'd like to leave it that way. The end." I hoped to end the conversation there.

"It doesn't matter who it was. All that matters is that you're here," Kenzie reminded.

"So," I began, taking a deep breath. "I've been doing a lot of thinking lately, and I've decided to get my own apartment."

Shelly's eyes widened. "How? Where?"

"Chase's parents are renting out their side apartment."

"How will you pay rent?"

"They don't want any money from me. I spoke to them this morning."

I couldn't read her expression. The girls sat quietly, waiting for her response.

"I feel really bad about staying at your place," I continued. "You say that it's fine, but I know you were planning on asking Brody to move in with you before this all happened. I don't want to hold you back from anything."

"You're not holding me back," she stated. "You do whatever you want to do, but just know that you can stay with me for as long as you need to."

"I know. Thank you for that."

The first few strums of the guitar signaled that the band was ready, and the room erupted in screams. Girls positioned themselves right in front of the stage, undoubtedly trying to be noticed. The lights dimmed, and only the spotlights at the bottom of the stage illuminated the band. Chase unclipped the microphone from the stand, and walked towards the edge of the small stage. The screams got louder as he raised the microphone to his mouth.

"Big Nose Kate's, it's Friday night! Are you ready?"

The crowd's cheers answered his question.

Chase began singing and I immediately recognized the first verse of my favorite Journey song. I watched him move around the stage with such confidence, singing effortlessly in front of the full room. It really should not have surprised me, since he was just as charismatic off stage. In that moment, I understood why girls had always treated him like he was a rock star, though I'd never admit it to him. His voice had just the right combination of smoothness and rasp, perfect for the genre of songs he performed. He jumped up and down to the beat while everyone in the bar sang along.

The guitarist stepped forward to perform his solo, and Chase hopped off the stage. The crowd cleared a path as he ran towards the bar and climbed on top. His eyes were fixed on mine while he sang, slowly stepping over people's drinks. My heart raced faster as I became more nervous with each step he took. When he had reached where I was sitting, he knelt down and belted out the chorus one last time. Shelly put her arm around me, and we sang along into her beer bottle. He winked at me before leaping off the bar to return to the stage.

My eyes remained glued to Chase for the duration of his set. It was intriguing to watch this other side of him. Had I seen him perform prior to getting to know him, I would have viewed him as nothing more than an attention-whore who was full of himself. Now, I was able to see how happy performing truly made him. I felt saddened knowing that he gave up on his dream for his family.

"I'll be right back," I shouted to the girls. I headed to the bathroom while everyone's attention was still on the stage. A window was cracked open in the stall, and there was a slight chill in the air. Summer weather was quickly disappearing, and it felt good compared to the stifling bar. While I was finishing up at the sink, a parade of half-naked girls burst through the door, which signaled that the band's first set had ended.

"He looked at me while he was singing that last song, did you see?" one girl boasted.

"Totally," the others agreed.

"That boy is lickable." The first one reapplied lip gloss, and blew herself a kiss in the mirror. I rolled my eyes as I tossed the paper towel into the trash.

When I emerged, the bar was crammed with people trying to get refills before the next set. I pushed my way through, as best as I could while protecting my sling.

"Merritt Adams!" An already drunk Shawn was shouting my name as he stumbled in front of me.

"Hey. Happy birthday, Shawn."

He hit the arm of his friend standing next to him. "Look who it is, Larry."

Larry's eyes widened. "Holy shit! Merritt Adams."

"I told you she wasn't dead, bro." Shawn wrapped his arm around me, leaning almost all of his weight on my shoulder. "He thought you were dead after that accident on the news."

I winced and tried to squirm out from under his arm. "Get off, you're hurting me."

"You look pretty damn good for a dead girl!" He was slurring his words into my ear as I pushed him away. Suddenly, Shawn released me as he was yanked backwards by the collar of his shirt.

Chase spun Shawn in the opposite direction, sending him back into the crowd.

"Are you okay?"

"Yeah. I guess nobody was expecting me since I'm supposed to be dead and all."

"Just ignore him. Is your arm okay?"

"It's fine. I shouldn't be here."

"Of course you should." He motioned to the dance floor. "Want to dance?"

I shook my head.

Chase started to shake his arms from side to side and gyrate his hips in a circle, all while wiggling his eyebrows wearing a goofy expression on his face. "Are you sure?"

I could not contain my laughter at the sight of his ridiculous dance. "With moves like that, I'm sure you can find someone else to dance with."

He moved his dancing closer to me. "I don't want to find someone else. I want to dance with you."

The closer he got, the harder I laughed. "Stop, Chase! You look like a crazy person."

He finally stopped. His expression changed as he looked into my eyes. As close as we were, I knew I could not let myself get sucked into his mesmerizing stare. I lowered my gaze, but quickly discovered that looking at his lips was no better. He pressed his body against mine, wrapping his arms around me so I could not escape. It was not aggressive or forceful, like the drunken Shawn from before; it was gentle and warm in his embrace. Plus, Chase smelled much better.

"Your friends are probably waiting for you." I tried to distract him.

"So let them wait."

I put my hand on his chest and lightly pushed him back. "Chase…"

He dropped his arms and took a step back. I could tell he was trying to hide a disappointed expression.

"I'm sorry. I promise I owe you a dance once the sling is off."

"Okay. I'll hold you to that, you know."

"I know."

He escorted me safely to the girls who were holding my seat at the bar.

"You sound great up there!" Shelly shouted.

I nodded in agreement. "You do."

His eyes lit up. "You think so?"

I motioned to the girls standing in waiting a few feet behind him. "You even got your own groupies."

He didn't turn around to look. "So, what's the verdict? Do I sound as good as Perry?"

"It's a close call."

He grinned. "I'm glad you came out tonight."

"So are we," Tina interjected. "Who knew all we had to do was send Chase Brooks over to convince you to come out of hiding."

I raised my middle finger in her face.

"Chase!" One of his bandmates called over to him from a table across the room. "Let's go!"

"I'm being summoned." He flashed me a smile before returning to his friends.

"He really likes you, Merr," Kenzie said gently. "I don't know if you're interested, but he definitely is."

"We're just friends."

"If you have to keep stating that you're just friends – you're not," Tina stated bluntly.

Shelly nodded, but said nothing. She knew better than to jump on this bandwagon.

"Maybe the time isn't right for you yet, but it will be." Kenzie was always the peacemaker of the group. I appreciated her softness. "You won't feel this way forever. You will feel better."

I was not so sure of that. I didn't know how to get past the things that had happened to me and act like everything could be good ever again. It was hard enough waking up to find out that I had been in a coma for almost two weeks. I was confused, and it took a while to remember the events that had led to that moment in the hospital bed. I had completely too much to drink, and crashed head-on into a tree. As I recalled why I was drunk in the first place, the unwanted memories came flooding back: I had showed up wasted to my father's funeral – my father was dead. I couldn't bear the pain. Nothing was normal; nothing made sense.

Everyone kept telling me that I would feel better in time, but when you're waiting to feel better, time feels like your worst enemy. What does "better" even mean? When grieving an unexpected loss, how do you feel better, exactly? All I wanted was for everything to go back to the way it used to be. It's like an eternal feeling of wanting to go home, but never actually getting there. I'm stuck searching for that sense of comfort, not knowing if I'll ever feel it again.

I tried to be okay for Shelly tonight. I tried to put on a brave face, but being around people made me more depressed. Luckily, Chase's next set began. I enjoyed the music almost as much as I enjoyed watching him in his glory on stage. He served as a diversion from any and all other thoughts.

When the show was over, he and his bandmates began packing up their equipment.

Shelly stood, holding Brody's hand. "Do you mind if I stay at Brody's tonight? Chase can drop us there, and then take you back to my apartment."

"Of course I don't mind. You don't have to ask my permission."

"Goodnight, bitches." Tina hugged me. "Don't be a stranger."

"Please call so we can hang soon, okay?" Kenzie was next to hug me.

"Sure."

Shelly, Brody, and I waited for Chase as the rest of the bar cleared out. Two girls stood next to the stage trying to talk to Chase. They were both blonde, one tall and one short.

"Look," Shelly pointed. "Let's get closer so we can hear what they're saying."

"I don't want to get up until I absolutely have to," I whined. "I haven't been out in a while and I forgot how exhausting it is."

"They looked like they got raped by a Macy's makeup counter." Shelly's face was twisted in disgust.

They were wearing a ton of makeup. I wondered if Chase found either one attractive.

"Look at Chase," Shelly continued, reading my mind. "He looks completely uninterested, and they just keep on talking."

"Maybe we should go save him," Brody agreed. "He's barely even looking at them while he packs up."

They both looked at me expectantly.

"Fine," I grumbled. As we got closer, I could hear their conversation.

"You were so good tonight," the short one said.

"Yeah. So good. You have an amazing voice," said the taller blonde.

"You should totally be famous," the short one said.

"Thanks," he replied without looking up, wrapping up the cord to the microphone. His eyes lit up when I stopped next to them. "You guys ready?"

"Sure, unless you're not finished with your conversation here." I looked at the girls and leaned towards them. "Wasn't he good tonight?"

"So good," the short one answered, while the other nodded fervently. They were completely clueless.

Shelly buried her head in Brody's chest to hide her laughter.

I smiled at Chase innocently. "You're just so good."

He shot me a look, and tossed his keys to Brody. "Why don't you pull my car around front? I'm all finished here, just have to carry this out to the van."

I turned to follow them when Chase grabbed my hand. "Walk with me."

The girls looked disappointed as we walked past them.

I giggled. "What's wrong? You didn't want to have a threesome with Tweedle dumb and Tweedle dumber?"

"Hardly."

"Why not? It would have been so good," I mimicked.

One corner of his mouth turned up.

"Dumb and blonde. Keeping the stereotype alive." I shook my head. "Shelly's sleeping over Brody's tonight. Do you mind dropping them off before taking me back to her place?"

"Of course not."

I yawned, watching as he loaded the last of the equipment into the back of the van. He swung the doors closed, and gave the bumper a tap. Ben, the drummer, stuck his hand out the window and waved before pulling away. We waited for Brody to pull the car around.

"You're really talented, Chase. You guys were great tonight."

He smiled, giving me a sideways glance. "Thanks."

"You looked so happy up there. How did you feel?"

He ran his fingers through his hair, which was damp from sweat. "It felt great. I know I shouldn't feel this way, but I wish I could have it all. I wish I could do what I love while staying here taking care of my family at the same time."

"I wish you could, too. You deserve to have it all. I'm sorry you had to leave California."

He looked down as Brody pulled up in front of us. "Everything happens for a reason, right?"

"If you say so."

Chapter Six: New Apartment

"Come on, get up. You need to get dressed."

"For what?" I rubbed my eyes sleepily.

Shelly put her hands on her hips. "We're going shopping for my party. Please tell me you haven't forgotten?"

"You're throwing a party?"

"Don't make jokes! This is an important event!"

I hoisted myself out of the recliner. "How could I forget the national holiday that is your birthday?"

I quickly threw on a t-shirt and yoga pants, and brushed my teeth as Shelly helped sweep my hair up in a bun. Her birthday was the day before Halloween. Every year, Brody's fraternity hosted a Halloween party at their house, and Shelly pretended it was her very own birthday extravaganza. The last thing I wanted to do was dress up in an uncomfortable costume, but for my best friend's birthday – I would have to put my own issues aside. She deserved an entire night of fun, and I refused to let my downward spiral ruin any of it for her. I just hoped my sling would be off by then.

"So, when do you move into Chase's apartment?" she asked as we navigated through the crowded mall.

"His parent's apartment," I corrected. "And they said it would be ready the end of this week." I wasn't sure what they needed to do in order to get it ready. According to Chase, the apartment was furnished and vacant.

"It's really great of them to let you stay, free of charge."

"I know. I'm not crazy about the idea. I've been racking my brain for ways to repay them, but I'm not coming up with much."

"It's too bad you're in the sling. You loved working on cars with your dad. You could have offered to help out at their shop."

My eyes lit up and the wheels in my mind started spinning. "That's not a bad idea." I began making a mental list of the things I could manage with one hand, for now.

"When will you be able to take the sling off for good?"

"They don't have a definite date, yet. Soon, I'm hoping. I guess it depends on how therapy goes."

"I hope you have it off in time for my party. I want your costume to look flawless!"

"Everything will be perfect for your party, just like always."

"Okay," she began when we stepped inside the costume store. "We need something cute, but not overdone. It can be funny, but not cliché."

"I know the drill," I reassured her.

We turned the corner of the first aisle to find Brody and Chase standing before us. I was going to shoot Shelly an angry look for not telling me we would have company on our shopping spree, but reminded myself that this was all for her birthday. On the plus side, Chase being there would stop Shelly from talking about him.

She pecked Brody on the cheek. "Let's get started."

"Hello to you, too." Chase was clearly amused at Shelly's seriousness. I hadn't been able to warn him ahead of time. The less we said, the better this would go.

"Hi. Start looking for a costume." She began rummaging through the first rack.

"Why don't we split up?" Chase suggested.

"No way. If we split up, you boys will pick something completely ridiculous. We stick together."

I looked at the costumes hanging nearby, and pretended not to notice Chase saluting her out of the corner of my eye.

"Do you still hate Halloween?" Brody asked me.

"Whoa. How can you hate Halloween?" Chase asked incredulously. "There's candy, parties, and scary movies!"

I rolled my eyes. "It's beyond stupid. What are we even celebrating? Guys can wear whatever costume they want, but girls are expected to dress in a totally absurd outfit that inevitably begins with the word 'sexy.'" I motioned to the costumes hanging on the shelf in front of us. "Sexy cop. Sexy maid. Sexy kitten. I mean, how the hell is a kitten sexy, anyway?"

Brody stifled a laugh, out of fear that Shelly would hear him. "She's got a point."

"Don't agree with her," Shelly teased. "Halloween is just supposed to be fun! It's a night to dress up like someone you aren't, and break out of your shell a little."

"I love it when girls break out of their shells, don't you?" Chase nudged Brody.

Shelly shot him a look.

I pushed him toward the next aisle. "Nothing good ever comes after that look."

We scoured the store, each picking up a costume for Shelly to deny. She was on a mission, and only she would know when she found what she was looking for.

"Khloe wants me to be a moose," Chase stated.

I scrunched my nose up. "A moose?"

"She's going to be Anna, from Frozen. So she wants me to be Sven."

"Anna? I like the kid already. Every girl always wants to be Elsa, but it was really Anna who was the hero."

"Yea, she's one kickass little girl. She takes after her awesome big brother, of course." He grinned proudly and pretended to dust off his shoulder.

"Who, Tanner?"

"You should be a comedian for Halloween since you're so funny."

I smiled and walked down the last aisle. "So, I have an idea how I can repay your parents for letting me stay in the apartment."

"I already told you. You don't have to repay them for anything."

I put up my hand. "Just hear me out. I know a lot about cars right?"

"Right."

"I used to work on cars with my dad growing up. I know I can't do any heavy lifting right now, but I can do other things in the meantime."

"You want to help out at the shop?"

I nodded and awaited his response. "What do you think?"

"We could definitely use the help. My dad's been… low on energy lately."

Shelly turned abruptly down the aisle and handed me a costume.

I held it up. "A flapper costume?"

"They can dress like flappers, and we can be gangsters," Brody said, handing a costume to Chase.

"We can get cigars," Chase thought out loud. "And guns!"

"Let's go see what they have." Brody and Chase disappeared into the back of the store.

I shook my head. "Boys and their toys."

"So what do you think?" Shelly asked eagerly. "Will you wear this?"

The model on the package was wearing a silver dress with tiers of fringe. It was short, but not too revealing. It was classy. "Sure. This looks okay."

She squealed. "Let's go look at their wig selection. I saw this blonde one with pin curls that I just need to have."

"Then have it you shall, my friend." I swung my arm around her shoulders as we walked towards the wigs.

"The boys are going to look so handsome in their gangster outfits."

I nodded in agreement.

"Chase is going to the party with you. That's kind of like a date, wouldn't you say?"

I picked up a short black bob, completely ignoring her question. "What about this one?"

"It's perfect! It will go great with your silver dress."

"Good. Here's your blonde one. Let's pay and get out of here."

A voice from behind me shouted, "Put your hands up where I can see 'em!"

I felt what I knew to be a toy gun pressed against my back. I slowly lifted my arm in the air and turned around to see Chase wearing a fedora hat with a fake cigar in his mouth.

"What do you think of the hat?"

"Honestly, those hats remind me of Freddy Krueger."

He grinned. "I think it makes the outfit." He tipped it over one eye.

"It will go perfectly with your costume," Shelly said excitedly.

I waited in line while Brody paid for his and Shelly's costumes.

"Next!" the cashier called.

I placed my costume on the counter, and Chase put his right next to mine.

"Together?" the cashier asked.

"Separate."

"Together," he answered, and handed her his credit card.

"Chase, no. Brody paid for Shelly's because he's her boyfriend. You don't have to pay for mine."

"Aww sweetie, you should let him pay for you! He's being such a gentleman," the cashier cooed. She was wearing fuchsia lipstick, the way old ladies always seemed to, and her name was etched onto her nametag in gold letters.

I grimaced. "Thanks a lot, Karen," I muttered under my breath.

"Yea sweetie." Chase grinned as he draped his arm around me. "I'm being a gentleman."

I rolled my eyes and shook him off. When he finished paying, we left the store with our new costumes.

"If you're paying for my costume, then I'm buying the movie tickets."

"What movie?" Shelly questioned.

"We're supposed to see the new Marvel movie tonight."

"Fine. You can get the tickets tonight," Chase agreed.

I gave him a skeptical look. That seemed too easy.

He grinned. "I'll pick you up at six."

Shelly kissed Brody goodbye, and we turned to walk back to her car. I pretended not to see her beaming next to me out of the corner of my eye.

"Say nothing," I warned her.

She held her hands up innocently. "I didn't say a word."

"You were thinking it! I can hear it."

"Dude, how are you this oblivious? He spends all his free time with you. What more proof do you need that this guy is into you?"

"This is Chase Brooks we're talking about here. Think about it, Shell. He's not exactly shy guy. If he liked me, he'd say something."

"You're not so approachable. Just let me ask him."

"You will not ask him anything!"

She smirked. "You know that if I ask him, he's going to be totally honest and admit that he has feelings for you."

"Or you'll be totally off base, and make him not want to hang out with me anymore. We are just two people, who happen to be of the opposite sex, that enjoy each other's company. Why is that so hard for you to accept?"

"It wouldn't be hard to accept if I didn't know you had feelings for him, too. You can't just be friends with someone you have feelings for. You taught me that, remember?"

"Do not compare this to your situation with Brody. Also, don't you think I would know if I had feelings for him? Don't you think I would tell you, of all people?"

She shook her head feverishly. "You're too scared to get involved with someone. You have this wall up because you don't want to get hurt, so you tell yourself that you don't have feelings for him. Lower that wall and maybe you'll be able to see what everyone else sees."

"Or," I held up one finger. "Everyone else sees what they want to see, because they're all so concerned with trying to make me happy again."

"Is there something wrong with us wanting to see you happy after everything you've just gone through?"

"No. I just… I need some time."

"I hate seeing you like this. I want you to have something good in your life. You've been through more than anyone should."

"As long as I have you, I will be fine. Just stop trying to make me and Chase a thing."

She sighed. "Fine. Just as long as you admit one thing."

I raised a skeptical eyebrow at her.

"Just admit that you find him attractive – for me! You cannot be the only girl on this planet that does not think he's gorgeous. I refuse to believe it!"

I laughed. "Of course I think he's attractive. Anyone with working eyeballs can see that he is beautiful. Scientists should conduct a study on his whole family... replicate their DNA or something."

"How are they that good looking? It's not normal."

"I'm sticking with my theory from fourth grade. They're aliens."

Shelly and I spent the rest of the day together, until I heard Chase's engine roar outside at six o'clock.

"He's here!" I shouted into the hallway.

"Wait! Let me see you!"

I rolled my eyes as she burst out of the bathroom to survey my outfit for approval.

Her grin spread from ear to ear. "You look nice."

"Can I go now?"

"You may. Have fun."

Chase was leaning against his car, the passenger door already opened. His arms were crossed over his chest, making his upper body appear even bigger than it already was. He was a walking Abercrombie ad. I could never deny that he was attractive, but that was easier to ignore back when I did not know him. Now, his personality only made him appear more perfect. I averted my eyes from his body parts as I approached him.

"Wow."

I raised an eyebrow. "Wow, what?"

"Wow, you. You look great."

I looked down at my outfit. A t-shirt with jeans tucked into boots signaled the fall weather had officially arrived. "I must have looked pretty shitty this summer if you're wowed over this."

"This," he gestured, "deserves to be wowed over – no matter what you're wearing. Your Cookie pajamas were cute, but I am a sucker for tight jeans."

"I think you're a sucker for whoever is inside of tight jeans." I slid into the passenger seat.

He leaned in to clip my seatbelt. "I'm really just a sucker for whatever pants you're inside of." His cologne wafted into my nostrils as he lingered, his lips inches from mine. He backed out and closed the door with a smirk on his face.

His advances were bolder lately – and harder to ignore. Determined to change the subject, I looked out the window at the menacing sky. "I hope those clouds hold off until we're inside the theatre."

"I love the rain. It's calming."

"It is perfect movie weather."

When we pulled up, the line for tickets was winding out the door. The only parking spots available were at the far end of the parking lot. He shifted the car into park. Then, the sky opened up.

I groaned.

"We have some time. Let's see if we can wait it out."

We waited, and waited, but the rain did not relent.

"Okay. Look, don't be mad," he started. "I have a confession to make. Promise you won't be mad?"

I turned to face him. "Mad? Why would I be mad?"

"Well, I checked the movie times earlier and saw that this movie was selling out fast. So I ordered the tickets online."

"And why would that make me mad?"

"At the mall earlier you said you wanted to pay for the tickets. I didn't want you to be angry, thinking I ignored you and paid for them anyway."

I looked down at my lap. Had I really been that difficult?

"What?"

"Of course you got the tickets ahead of time. It was selling out. I'm glad you did."

"I wasn't sure if I should, but then we wouldn't be able to see the movie tonight. I didn't want you to be disappointed."

"Chase, it's fine. Really. Thanks for doing that. I can get the snacks, how's that?"

He smiled and relaxed into his seat. "Sure."

"Let's just get inside. I don't think this rain is stopping any time soon."

He reached into the back seat and pulled out an umbrella. He ran around the car and held the door open for me. When I got out, he pulled me in close.

"You want to make a run for it?"

I nodded. "On your mark…"

"Go!" he shouted.

I tried to keep up with him, while he tried to keep the umbrella covering the both of us. My arm was wrapped tightly around his. We were both laughing until we approached the curb. A huge puddle had formed, and we were heading straight for it.

"Chase," I warned, trying to slow down.

"You can make it!"

"Chase! My legs aren't long enough!"

"Jump, now!"

We both leapt over the puddle. I squeezed his arm as he pulled me across. We were out of breath, and still laughing when we landed on the other side.

"I would have killed you if I landed in that puddle!"

"You have no faith in me." He held out his arm. "Look at these little claw marks you left in me. It looks like I got attacked by a baby squirrel."

"I couldn't exactly pay attention to my grip as I was flying through the air." I rubbed his arm for good measure. "You'll live."

We blew past the line and scanned our tickets on Chase's phone at the machine. Then, we stood in front of the snack counter and surveyed the options.

"So, are you a chocolate or gummy kind of girl?"

"Both. What kind of question is that?" I reached out and took a bag of Sour Patch Kids along with a box of Junior Mints. "What are you getting?"

He chuckled. "Oh, are those all for you?"

"I don't share my snacks."

"Not even with me?!"

I shook my head. "Not even with the one and only Chase Brooks."

He grabbed a large bag of popcorn off the shelf. "Fine. Then you can't have any of my popcorn."

"Fine."

"Do you guys want drinks?" the cashier asked.

I looked at Chase.

"Just get one, and we can share."

I hesitated. "Just one. Large, I guess."

"Enjoy your movie!"

I took my change and the cup from the cashier, and walked to the soda fountains. "What are we drinking?"

Chase shrugged. "Whatever you want."

"Grab some napkins." I pointed to the popcorn surrounding his feet on the floor. "You look like you're going to need a bunch."

He shoveled a giant-sized handful of popcorn into his mouth. Pieces dropped everywhere. "You think?"

I couldn't help but laugh. "Maybe see if they have a tarp instead."

Inside the theatre buzzed with excitement. I noticed several familiar faces. I ducked my head behind Chase until we found our way to our seats in the back.

"Crowded in here," he commented.

"Good thing you got our tickets ahead of time."

He watched as I tried to adjust myself comfortably in the reclining seat. "I can move this armrest up if you need more room."

"No, I'm okay." I gave him a side look. "I need a barrier to keep you from my snacks."

He dramatically covered his tub of popcorn. "Then keep your grubby hands off my corn!"

"Hey, Brooks!" someone shouted.

Chase looked up to see one of our old high school classmates approaching from the row in front of us. His face looked familiar, but I could not for the life of me remember his name.

"Hey, Eric. How's it going?"

"It's going well, my man. How was California? I'm surprised you're back already."

I cringed. He must have to deal with that a lot. I wondered if he felt embarrassed.

"California was good. It's nice to be back home, though."

Eric realized I was sitting next to Chase, and did a double-take. "Merritt? How the hell are you?"

"I'm good."

"Wow. I saw your accident on the news. I can't believe you're alive."

"Here I am."

"It was good to see you, Eric," Chase intercepted. "Enjoy your movie."

Luckily, Eric took the hint and waved goodbye. "Take care, guys."

My polite smile turned into a sneer once his back was turned.

Chase laughed while he shook his head. "People don't get it. It's not their fault."

"No. I blame their parents for making them so stupid."

"Eventually, everyone will forget about you, and me, and move on to the next big story."

"Can't wait," I muttered as the lights turned down. If I was going to be in public, at least I was safe in the darkness.

Thirty minutes into the movie, I had already finished both boxes of my candy. Chase's hand slowly reached over for the chocolate. I stared straight ahead, pretending not to notice, and allowed him to take the empty box off my lap. I could see his confused expression as he shook the box into his hand and nothing came out. I started giggling.

He leaned over and whispered, "You ate everything already?!"

I tried to be quiet as I laughed. He tossed a handful of popcorn at me, which only made me laugh more.

I reached out my hand. "Can you pass me the drink?"

"Nope."

"Hand it over."

He crossed his arms over his chest and relaxed back into his seat with a grin on his face.

I could not reach it with the armrest in between us. I slowly lifted it up, and scooted over. I tried to stretch my arm across him.

"Aww you want to snuggle?" He put his arm around me and squeezed so that I could not move from my spot.

I squirmed trying to reach the soda.

Finally, he gave in and handed me the cup. I took a few swigs and dug my elbow in his side while he whimpered quietly. I handed the cup back to him and went to slide back over to my side.

"Stay here," he whispered, holding onto me. "I'm comfortable."

I hesitated for a moment.

"Stay," he breathed into my ear again. He was warm and smelled like popcorn. It was oddly comforting to feel him beside me in the seat.

I reluctantly sat back. I felt stiff, but didn't dare move for fear of what his next move might be. I focused my attention straight ahead.

We remained like that for the duration of the movie until the credits started scrolling across the screen.

I quickly sat up as the lights came back on. "What did you think?"

"It was great. You?"

I nodded in agreement. "I liked it."

We walked out with the masses, and made our way back to the car. Luckily, the rain had subsided.

"If you could be any superhero, who would you be?"

He smiled as he started the engine. "That's easy. Superman."

"I knew you were going to say that."

"Why's that?"

"I don't know. I could see it. I'm just glad you didn't say Batman."

"What do you have against Batman?"

"He doesn't have any real superpowers! He's just a guy with gadgets. What if something doesn't work one day, or his batteries die? There he is, scaling down a building – boom. Dead. He is one faulty piece of equipment away from being roadkill. And Spiderman – don't even get me started. Who wants to shoot webs out of their hands?! That's disgusting."

Chase was laughing. "Who would you be? The Hulk?"

"No. That's really not ideal. I would be Phoenix."

"As in Gene Grey, turn evil and kill everyone Phoenix?"

"Yup. I would be able to move shit with my mind. I could hear what everybody was thinking. She was the most powerful."

"Would you read my mind?"

"I wouldn't have to. You're an easy read."

"You think so, huh?"

I noticed we weren't on the way to Shelly's apartment. "Hey, where are we?"

"I want to show you something."

"So we're not going back to Shelly's?"

"We're making a pit stop first."

I sat quietly trying to figure out where we were headed. The neighborhood looked familiar when he slowed down. Larger homes, perfectly manicured lawns. This was the nicer side of town. Then he pulled into a driveway.

I looked up at the white colonial before me. There were more windows in one room than I had in my whole house. The largest window above the front door displayed a spiral staircase and a crystal chandelier.

"This is your house, isn't it?"

He grinned. "Come see your new apartment."

I quickly followed him up the driveway. "Are your parents home?"

"Why are you whispering?"

"I don't know." I looked around. "What time do they go to bed?"

He chuckled as he led me up the concrete stairs on the side of the house. "You don't have to worry about what they are doing. You come and go as you please. This is your own place."

At the top landing, he turned around and handed me a key. "This is yours."

I turned the key in the lock and pushed open the door. I looked for a light switch along the wall. Chase flicked the lights on behind me. The bright white walls smelled like they were freshly painted. In the living room, there was a three-seat gray couch with a matching single recliner facing a flat screen television mounted on the wall. The room was open to the small eat-in kitchen, with stainless steel appliances. The glass kitchen table seated four people. I turned and followed the hallway to find a small pale blue bathroom with a walk-in shower. The room next to it was the bedroom. There was a dresser, bed, and desk, all pushed into the center of the room covered by clear plastic.

"We wanted you to pick the color for your bedroom. Then I can paint it for you before you move in this weekend."

I stood in awe of the place. Everything looked brand new. I walked back into the living room to take another look.

"Well?" Chase was right behind me. "What do you think of your new home?"

Home. The word was foreign to me. "You know, I always had to worry about taking care of my dad. My whole life. I never imagined what it would be like to move out of the house and live on my own. I never thought about having my own place."

"You deserve everything you want in life. You can have whatever you want."

Looking in his eyes, it seemed believable. I felt a pounding in my chest.

"What's wrong?"

"It's… beautiful in here. I love it."

"You've been through enough. It's time you start feeling what it's like to be happy."

"Maybe we could go check out some paint colors tomorrow?"

His eyes lit up with excitement. "Definitely."

"Maybe I could help you paint, too."

"Whatever you want to do. You just say the word."

On the ride back to Shelly's, hundreds of emotions surged throughout my body at once. I was in a daze when Chase pulled to a stop and turned off the engine.

"You okay in there?" he asked quietly.

I nodded, and offered him a smile. "Tonight was fun."

He reached out and stroked my cheek with his thumb. "I like spending time with you. I like being with you."

I gently pulled his hand away from my face, and gave it a squeeze before placing it in his lap. "Ditto. I'll see you tomorrow."

I got out of the car before he could say another word. It was a great night, and I didn't want anything to ruin it.

Chapter Seven: Dinner with the Brooks

"How can there be so many whites? Isn't white just... white?"

Chase chuckled. "There are a lot of different shades."

"Could you imagine being one of those people? Darling, do you think we should go with the off-white, or the egg white?"

"I don't know, darling. What about the vanilla white?" His accent was almost worse than mine.

"That one is a bit whiter than the other white."

"Darling, this is such a tough decision."

"This white really brings out the white in your eyes, darling."

We were laughing when a worker approached us. "Do you kids need any help finding a color?"

Chase wrapped his arm around me. "We are looking for the perfect color for my darling's bedroom."

I shook his arm off, trying to stop laughing. "I don't want something too loud. Not sure on the actual color."

The old man handed me a few paint swatches. "These are really popular in the bedroom."

"Thanks."

Chase leaned in as the man walked away. "I bet he knows exactly what's popular in the bedroom." He wiggled his eyebrows.

"Ew. So not what I wanted to picture." I shuffled through the swatches until I found a pale yellow color. I held it up. "What do you think of this one?"

Chase nodded. "I like it. It's happy."

"It's called A Hint of Sunshine."

"It suits you."

I laughed. "What does that even mean?"

"You seem so sad and guarded on the outside. But once in a while, you smile, and it's like a hint of sunshine comes across your face, just for a moment."

"That's good. You should call Hallmark and get that on a card."

We picked out paint brushes and rollers while we waited for the cans to be shaken. When it was ready, we carried everything to the checkout counter.

Chase stepped in front of me. "This is being taken care of, so don't even take out your wallet."

"No, no. This paint is for my room, so I'm going to pay for it."

"Nope. Beverly's orders. This is all part of getting your apartment ready. She would be painting for any tenant that moved in."

I sighed. "I guess you being difficult runs in your family, huh?"

"Oh, and she wants you to come to dinner tonight. After we finish painting."

I tried to hide my unease.

Once we were back at the apartment, Chase began laying out all of the materials. I set up my phone to play the best of the eighties while we painted. There was no conversation, which was nice for a change. We hummed along to a song every now and then. Painting felt therapeutic. The sound of the paint brushes swishing up and down was calming. It didn't hurt that I got to steal a glance or two at Chase while he worked. He had muscles in his arms that I didn't even know existed, as they contracted with every push and pull of the roller. I also happened to notice the way his shorts curved around his perfectly round rump. I was foolishly staring when he unexpectedly turned around.

"How does it look from down there?"

"What?"

"The paint. How does it look?"

I bit my bottom lip to keep from laughing. "It's perfect."

He nodded in agreement. "We'll let it dry, and paint the second coat in the morning. It will be ready for you to sleep here by tomorrow night."

I glanced at the time on my phone. Two hours had gone by like seconds. "I'd better jump in the shower to get ready for dinner."

"See you at six." He gave me a wink and carried away the brushes and rollers.

When I heard the door close, I typed out a text to Brody: I need a big favor - can you drop off a bottle of wine outside my apartment please?

I hit send and stepped into the shower. I refused to show up to dinner emptyhanded with the Brooks family, and Chase would have told me that wine was not necessary. How I was counting the days until I could be rid of this sling, and drive wherever I wanted – even though I had nothing to drive. I put on jeans and a plain black V-neck shirt; I didn't want to look like crap, but I also didn't want to look like I was trying too hard. Dinner with the entire Brooks family was intimidating. I made a single-handed attempt to run some gel through my hair so the curls didn't look so frizzy. I smiled when I saw the bottle of wine sitting on my doorstep outside my front door. I walked down the stairs, across the front yard, and rang the doorbell next to the fancy giant double doors. Then, I took a deep breath.

To my surprise, a tiny blonde-haired human opened the door. "It's her!" she shouted. "Come in. Do you like my dress?" Khloe twirled and waited for my response.

I smiled as I stepped into the grandiose entryway. "I love it. Yellow is my favorite color."

"That's what Chase said. He is very excited you're coming to dinner. So is my mom. She said that Chase doesn't bring a lot of girls home, so this is big." Her hazel eyes widened to put emphasis on the last word.

I laughed as she took my hand and dragged me into the dining room.

"Chase! Look! Merry is here!"

Chase and his father were setting the table.

"It's Merritt, you knucklehead." Tanner waltzed into the room. He gave me a nod before sitting down to await the food.

"It's fine," I reassured Khloe. I could care less what she called me. I walked over to Tim and handed him the bottle of wine. "I wasn't sure what to bring."

Chase smiled and shook his head while Tim gave me a hug. He still smelled like the shop. It reminded me of my father. "That was very kind of you. You didn't have to bring anything."

Beverly appeared in the doorway from the kitchen. "You did not have to bring a single thing. This is your special dinner."

"I don't need a special dinner. The apartment is more than enough. I don't know how I can ever repay you for everything."

"I should be the one getting a special dinner. You took my apartment," Tanner grumbled.

I had to stop my jaw from dropping open. "What do you mean?"

Chase smacked him in the back of the head. "You wish it was your apartment. I'm the older one, it would have been mine, if anything."

"You left for two years. I had dibs on it," Tanner retorted.

"Enough now!" Beverly entered the dining room carrying a large oven-baked chicken decorated on all sides with sliced potatoes. It smelled amazing. I could not remember the last time I had a home-cooked meal that I had not prepared myself.

Chase reserved the seat next to him for me, pulling out the chair.

"Thanks for telling me I was stealing your brother's apartment," I quietly gritted through my smile.

"You're sitting next to me, Merry!" she squealed.

"Oh, good!"

I watched everyone's interactions while Tim carved and served the chicken. It was such a normal family, if there even was such a thing, like one you'd see on a television sitcom. I had never had anything remotely close to this. The only family I had was my father, as dysfunctional as it was. I pushed the thought from my mind, and tried to remain in the moment.

"Merry, your hair is so pretty. Why is it so curly like that?" Khloe was twisting one of my curls around her finger.

"That's just the way it grows out of my head. My mom had curly hair, so I do too."

"Where is your mom? Why didn't she come to dinner with you?"

"Her mom lives very far away, sweetheart," Tim chimed in.

I gave him a grateful smile. He winked, and it looked just like Chase's wink.

"Just like you have the same hair as your mom and Chase." I patted her head.

"It's soft like his too. Feel it!"

I ran my fingers through her hair. "Your hair is very soft."

"Now feel Chase's hair."

Chase leaned onto my lap, and everyone laughed. I reluctantly ran my fingers through his hair, probably turning three different shades of red. "I think yours is even softer," I said to Khloe with wide eyes.

"Is not," scoffed Chase sitting back up.

"Is too!" she retorted.

"So, I hear you'll be working with us this week." Tanner barely looked up from his plate when he spoke to me.

He looked so different from Chase and Khloe. Shelly always referred to him as the dark brother. Chase had his father's eyes, but Tanner had Tim's complexion. Dark olive skin, dark eyes, still the same killer smile. He was not as outgoing as Chase, and had always gotten into trouble at school. If Chase was the rock star, Tanner was definitely the bad boy.

"I'll be there," I replied.

"Do you even know anything about cars?"

"Tanner," Chase warned.

"I do, actually. I used to help my dad restore his old classics."

"Restoring them and fixing them are two different things."

"Tanner, are you going somewhere with this?" This time Tim spoke up.

"Just making conversation."

"Your people skills are astounding," Chase countered.

"It's fine," I reassured. "I wouldn't want dead weight around the job either."

"See? She gets it." It was obvious that Tanner spent a lot of time having to defend himself.

"Well, it was very nice of you to lend your services," Beverly stated. She reached out and covered Tim's hand with hers. "We could use the extra help these days."

Chase reached over for my hand under the table. I wasn't sure if it was because he thought I would be reminded of my dad, or because he was the one who needed strength. I interlocked my fingers with his. I knew he would need all the strength he could get in the upcoming months. Tim looked more tired than the last time I had seen him, and it had only been a few days.

"Daddy has cancer. Do you know what cancer is, Merry?"

I nodded. "I do."

"Chase told us that your dad died. Our dad is going to die too."

The silence was louder than any sound I had ever heard. "My dad did die."

"Were you sad?"

"I was. I still am."

"Aww Merry." Khloe wrapped her arms around my midsection and squeezed tightly.

"Careful of her sling, dear." Beverly quickly dabbed her eye with her napkin while Khloe was distracted.

"How did you get this?" Khloe was full of questions. It was to be expected, as I was a newcomer and she was a child. I did not mind, or feel embarrassed. Everyone at the table knew my story, I assumed, and I didn't feel judged by them. They were warm and welcoming people. Well, maybe not Tanner so much.

"I got into a car accident. I was crushed up against the steering wheel, and hurt my shoulder."

Her eyes were wide. "Oh my gosh. Were you bleeding?"

"Enough questions," Tim said gently from across the table. "Let Merritt eat. You need to finish your vegetables, too."

Khloe scrunched up her face. "But I don't want broccoli."

I held up a piece of my broccoli. "Bet I can eat mine faster than you!"

Her frowning mouth turned into a devilish grin. "Ready? One, two, three!"

We both shoveled the broccoli into our mouths and tried to chew as fast as we could. I think even Tanner cracked a smile. This continued until her plate was clean.

"If you can get her to eat vegetables, you can come for dinner any time," Tim said.

"You are welcome here any time, Merritt. For dinner, or anything else you need. Consider yourself part of our family now."

I smiled. "Thank you. The same goes for you. I'm always here to help."

When had everyone finished eating, Beverly stood and began clearing off the table.

"Kokomo, go say goodnight. It's bath time." Tim walked out of the dining room towards the stairs.

"Can you come back again soon?" Khloe wrapped her arms around my legs and looked up at me with her big, round expectant eyes.

I knelt down and hugged her as tightly as I could with one arm. "Of course. I'll be living right next door, you know."

"Really?" She jumped up and down. "Can we have a sleepover?"

"You've done it now," Tanner said as he stood. "Now she'll want to come over every day."

"That's fine by me." I gave her one more squeeze. "Go enjoy your bath time with your dad."

It was heartbreaking to think that one day Tim wouldn't be around to give her baths. I silently vowed to help her through this. I'd help them all in any way I could.

Chase was waiting with his keys. "Come on. I know you're excited for your last night with Shelly. I'll drive you home."

Admittedly, I was disappointed to leave. It felt so good to be there. The kind of good I hadn't felt in a long time, if ever.

"Let me just bring the rest of this stuff to your mom." I walked into the kitchen with as much as I could carry in one arm to find Beverly loading the dishwasher. "I just wanted to thank you again. For everything."

She took the dishes from me and set them down. She turned and wrapped her arms around me, holding me there for a moment. "We are always here, any time you need anything. Please don't hesitate to ask." She lifted her hands to hold my face. "You are strong and brave. Chase needs someone like you in his life."

My eyes filled with tears as I saw her own tears spill down her cheeks. All I could do was nod.

"You keep thanking me," she continued. "But I can't thank you enough."

"Me? For what?"

"You can't imagine how terrible I felt that Chase had to come back home. As Tim's cancer progresses, it's going to be the hardest on him. But he's happy when he's with you. You bring life back to him. I'm so thankful he has you."

The tears were streaming down both of our faces now, in the middle of the kitchen.

"What is happening in here?" Chase stood in the doorway, looking afraid to take another step further.

"Oh, don't mind us." Beverly laughed while she wiped her eyes. "Have a good night, Merritt."

"Thanks again, for dinner." I ducked my head as I walked swiftly past Chase. I gave Tanner a wave, and walked out the front door. I didn't stop until I was inside the car.

"What was that all about?" Chase asked as he buckled himself in.

"It was… that was… a lot. For me."

He looked guilty as he stared straight at the road ahead.

"Your mom loves you so much. I hope you know that." I looked out the window and focused on the moon. "You're so lucky."

"She loves you now, too."

I wiped what I hoped would be the last escapee tear.

"I'm sorry Khloe asked so many questions. I know she brought up a lot of stuff you don't like talking about."

"She's just a kid. She doesn't know." I turned my head to look at him. "I absolutely adore her."

He grinned from ear to ear. "She adored you right back. You know you're going to have to have a sleepover with her. She won't forget."

"I totally don't mind."

When we arrived at Shelly's apartment, for the last official time, Chase put the car in park and unclipped me. "Enjoy your night. I'll swing by in the morning to get you. We can put the last coat of paint on."

"Shelly said she'd drop me over to you. She wants to see the apartment. I'll meet you there around nine."

"Okay. Sounds good." He looked down at his lap. "It was really nice having you at dinner tonight."

"It was nice being there."

"Yeah?"

"Yeah." We held each other's gaze in the silence of his car. I broke first and swung open the door, waving goodbye before swinging it shut.

I could hear Shelly squealing before I even set foot on the top step.

"Finally! I thought you forgot about me!"

I walked straight to the couch and dropped myself down. "Sorry, I'm sorry. I didn't want to be rude and run out as soon as dinner was over."

"How was it?"

"Can we not talk about it tonight? Just for tonight."

"Your eyelashes look flat."

"So?"

"So that means you were crying. Did Chase say something to make you cry?"

"No. Tomorrow, Shell. I promise you, tomorrow." There was no way I could put into words how I felt tonight after dinner with the Brooks family. My head was a racetrack of thoughts and emotions zipping faster around each turn. I needed to sort things out on my own before I could explain any of it.

She sighed dramatically. "Fine." She walked over to the kitchen table and picked up a bowl of popcorn, wedging two soda cans in each of her elbows. "Our movie night extravaganza begins! Which one do you want to watch first?"

I draped my legs over her lap after she sat, and took the popcorn bowl. "Dealer's choice."

"Thelma and Louise, it is."

"I don't even know why you bother asking."

"Shush. It's your last night here. You have to be nice to me."

I rested my head on her shoulder. "Fine. If I have to."

"I love you, Toad."

"I love you, Frog."

Chapter Eight: Surprise

"Wow." Shelly stared out her windshield with her mouth open. "Their house is so nice."

"Yeah. You're not kidding." I lead her up the driveway and up the stairs. "Here we are." I turned the key in my apartment door and pushed it open. The smell hit me before the realization did. I stood in the doorway, blinking, as two pairs of eyes looked back at me from inside my kitchen.

"Surprise!" Shelly shouted from behind me. She gave me a push to walk further inside.

"What's going on?"

Brody and Chase were standing in the kitchen, both of them smiling from ear to ear. A vase of colorful flowers dressed up the table set for four.

"We wanted to welcome you into your first official day at your apartment." Shelly pushed me towards a chair. "Brody's making your favorite breakfast."

"Wow, guys. Thanks. I wish my bedroom was done so I could show you the finished space."

Chase sat next to me, and piled three blueberry pancakes onto my plate. "Oh, your room is done. Want some juice?"

My eyebrows furrowed. "What do you mean the bedroom is done? We still have another coat to do."

"No, we don't."

I stood and made my way into the hallway, peering through the doorway. The furniture no longer sat in the middle of the room under plastic. Everything was placed perfectly in the room, with the bed situated in between the two windows. "Chase! It's all done!"

"I know." He appeared in the doorway.

I walked past the bed, running my hand along the puffy white comforter, over to the cream-colored dresser. I picked up a picture frame that had been placed there. It held my favorite picture of me and Shelly, taken after we had met on the first day of kindergarten. "You decorated, too?"

"That was me!" Shelly called from the kitchen.

The frame next to it displayed another one of my favorites. My father, in the cherry red Chevelle we had built together, with my eighteen-year old self grinning wildly from the driver's seat for the first time.

"I love your smile in that picture," Chase said.

I noticed the third picture frame was empty.

"That one is being saved for a picture of us."

"Oh, yeah?"

"You've got some old pictures there – important memories from your past. Now it's time to make some new memories – fun memories in your new life."

I turned around to look at him. His hair was messier than usual; he had undoubtedly woken up early to finish painting. Without him stepping into my life that day in the cafeteria, none of this would be happening. No apartment, no job. He would have remained the beautiful stranger he had always been. Instead, we stood in my new bedroom, in my new apartment. I would be starting my new job at the auto shop tomorrow. My sling would be off in a few weeks thereafter. It felt like everything was gradually, finally, going back to normal – a new normal. It felt like for the first time, I was in control of my life.

I walked towards him without saying a word, and burrowed my head into his chest. His arms wrapped around me and held me tight. A mere "thank you" would not say enough how grateful I was for him. He rested his chin on the crown of my head. I knew he understood.

"Come on, you two," Brody called. "Breakfast is getting cold."

I turned around just in time to catch Shelly smack his arm for interrupting us. I sat beside her at the table. "Is that my spatula? Do I own a spatula?"

"You are now the proud owner of a spatula. I'm so happy for you, Merritt." Brody smiled his toothy grin – the same smile that made me instantly want to be his friend ten years ago. "Your place looks great."

"It's perfect. Thank you guys, so much." I made eye contact with Chase across the table.

The four of us talked and laughed while we filled our stomachs with sugar and gluten. Brody always made the best pancakes. They were never burned or flat like when I attempted to make them; they were fluffy golden perfection.

After breakfast, the boys left. Shelly flopped onto the couch while I sprawled out on the recliner.

"This thing is comfortable. I need to get myself a sugar mama like Beverly."

I shook my head. "I feel so guilty staying there for free."

"Don't feel guilty. You deserve something nice for a change."

"Chase said the same thing."

She was quiet for a moment. "He cares about you, Merritt. Truly."

"I know."

The truth took her by surprise. She sat up. "You know?"

"I do. I just don't know what to do with it."

"You accept it. That's what you do. Let it in."

I stared up at the ceiling. "Do you remember when your parents took us to the Grand Canyon senior year?"

"Of course."

"Do you remember when we hiked up to the top of that one rocky area, and the tour guide wanted us to scale around it to the other side? My legs locked up and I couldn't move. He reached his hand out for me, and kept telling me to walk towards him."

"But you couldn't," she recalled.

"That's exactly how I feel lately. Everyone is trying to push me forward, but I'm too fear-stricken to move. I keep telling my legs to go, but they won't. So I remain exactly where I am – where it's safe."

"You can't stay still for the rest of your life. You need to keep moving forward. That's the only way you'll get through any of this." She squeezed herself into the chair beside me, wrapping both of her arms around me.

"How did everything get so screwed up?" I murmured.

"Life screws things up sometimes. I wish I knew why. But I have to believe that it makes us stronger."

"Well then I should be as strong as an ox by now."

She grabbed my face. "You are a warrior."

"Yeah, right. Just call me Xena."

"Xena the Warrior Princess!" She jumped to her feet. "Ayiyiyi!"

I laughed at her pathetic attempt at a battle cry. She continued to jump up and down until I was doubled over with laughter.

"I'm going to miss you," she admitted, plopping back down next to me.

"I'll only be a few minutes away. It's not like I'm leaving the state."

"I know. But it won't be the same."

"You'll be happy when Brody moves in. Which, I'm assuming, will be soon."

"This weekend."

"My little girl is all grown up, living with her boyfriend!"

"Don't try to change the subject. What are we going to do about your feelings for Chase?"

I groaned and covered my face with my hands.

"You'll have to tell him."

"There's nothing to tell. I'm Xena, remember? Warriors don't have boyfriends."

"Xena actually had a girlfriend, if I remember correctly."

"Well, I don't want one of those either."

"You know what scares me, Merr? I'm afraid you're going to push Chase so far into the friend zone that he's going to give up. And by the time you realize it all, it's going to be too late! What happens if he gets a girlfriend? What will you feel like then?"

The thought had not crossed my mind. "I don't know. If he wants a girlfriend, he should find one."

"He treats you like his girlfriend. He's falling for you, whether you acknowledge it or not. He knows you're going through a lot, and he's being patient right now, taking his time to not scare you away. Eventually, it's going to get old. He won't stay around forever."

"I can't rush myself into something if I'm not ready."

"You'll never start anything if you keep telling yourself that you're not ready. Just jump in, with both feet."

"I'm not like you, Shell."

"You owe it to yourself to try to be happy."

"The two most important people in my life left me – both parents made a conscious choice to abandon me. I'm not jumping to sign myself up for another loss."

She stood. "Forgive me for saying this, but you need to hear it: maybe you need to stop feeling sorry for yourself. All you do is mope around with this woe-is-me attitude. Believe me – I know more than anyone how awful things in your life have been. But when do you move on from them? When do you leave the past in the past instead of dragging it around everywhere with you? In case you haven't noticed, your life isn't shitty anymore! You're not stuck taking care of a mentally ill parent anymore. I know you miss him, and I do, too. But he was gone long before he died. Nothing can change what has happened – you sitting here alone won't change it. At least he isn't in pain anymore, and at least you can live your life without coming home every night to guilt and sorrow."

Tears stung my eyes. "I know I can't change anything. I tried as hard as I could to help him, but it wasn't enough. I wasn't enough. I wasn't enough to make either of my parents stay."

"Stop telling yourself that you aren't enough. Stop telling yourself that you don't deserve anything. You could have died in that car when you crashed. Someone rescued you. Someone gave you a second chance at your life. You are free now. So, your mother, wherever she is, can go screw herself! Take the good memories of your father and keep them in your heart forever. But stop feeling sorry for yourself, because you are free!" She was crying as she screamed the truth at me.

The impact of her words hit me like a wave, the kind that stuns you and knocks you off of your feet. It sounded insensitive – almost callous – to tell someone that she was free of her burdensome father now that he was dead. But I understood what it truly meant. Though I was heartbroken that he was gone, it was even more heartbreaking to watch him die inside while he was still alive. Shelly endured everything I had gone through in my life, and she knew better than anyone how it felt. Only she could say this to me.

I sobbed as I finally allowed myself to consciously admit that it was time to let go of it all – that it was relieving to no longer have the responsibility of caretaker.

"You know I'm right. All the guilt is weighing you down, like an anchor. You need to let that go. You're going to drown if you don't."

"Who feels glad that her parent is dead? I failed him. I tried to make him better, but I failed."

"You did not fail him. It was not your job to make him better. Nobody could make him better. He was sick. You're not glad that he's dead. You're relieved that you don't have to go through that torture anymore. It's a normal reaction. People go through this all the time with sick parents. This is how you embrace your freedom. This is how you begin to climb out of your depression. This is how you can finally live the life you have always wanted."

I knew she was right. There was nothing I could do to help my father, and I had tried everything. I had given up important years of my life, devoted to trying to make him happy and sane. It was too big for me. Sometimes, you can't help the people you love. It wasn't me who wasn't enough. Sometimes, love isn't enough.

"And you're forgetting one very important detail about that day at the Grand Canyon," she continued. "Don't you remember how you got around the side of that rock?"

I nodded. "You."

"Me. I got you through it. I always will."

She sat with me as I cried. As much as I hated crying, it felt like a weight was being lifted off of my entire being. They say admitting something is the first step to recovering from an addiction. Guilt is as strong an addiction as any; she forces your mind to become her handmaiden, creating thoughts and emotions that validate and perpetuate her. I felt guilt for my mother leaving; I felt guilt for not being able to fix my father's problems; I felt guilt for driving drunk; I felt guilt for destroying the car my father and I had built together; I felt guilt for feeling sadness. One thing lead to the next, and soon there were bridges connecting all thoughts and emotions, leading them back to the fortress of guilt. I had my time to wallow in it, but now it had begun to fill up my lungs and I was drowning in it. I could let myself sink, tied to the sandbags of depression, being dragged further and further down into to the depths. But Shelly had just handed me the knife, and all I had to do was cut myself free. I could fight my way to the surface.

I cried until the tears ran dry. Shelly eventually passed out next to me, and two hours later, I was awakening from a nap, too. Quietly, I tiptoed to the bathroom and closed the door. My eyes were red and puffy as I faced myself in the mirror. I tore everything off, let down my hair, and stepped into the shower. I let the cool water beat down onto my face while I sat at the bottom of the shower.

Chase flashed through my mind. He, too, would experience the way it feels to live a grief-stricken life. He will bear witness to the deterioration of his father, as well as carry the grief of his mother, and his family. I imagined what he would be like, and it broke my heart. I would not want him to give into the sadness and despair. I would not want him to be devoid of happiness and love. So, if I did not want that for him, why did I accept that fate for myself? Why did I think I was undeserving of anything good? Why could I take care of others so easily, but refuse to even try to care for myself? Questions swarmed my mind throughout my shower. When I turned off the water and stepped out onto the bathmat, a noise startled me out of my thoughts. I wrapped the towel around my body, and walked down the hallway as my hair dripped behind me.

"Dude, we totally passed out," I called to Shelly. "I can't remember the last time I cried like that." When I reached the living room, I let out a shriek. "What the hell are you doing in here?!"

Chase, who was sitting on my couch – not Shelly – jumped up. "I'm sorry! Shelly let me in when she was leaving."

I tightened the bath towel around me, clutching it to my body. "You can't just come in here while I'm in the shower!"

"I didn't know you were in the shower until I was already inside."

"Turn around! Get out of here!"

He walked slowly with a smirk. "You're all covered. There's nothing to see."

"Just go! And stop smiling!"

His smirk turned into a grin. "I'm sorry. I came to see if you needed anything."

"And you couldn't have sent that in a text?" I began pushing him towards the door.

He spun around to face me. "I mean, I already saw you. You might as well let me stay at this point."

"You are so–"

"Charming? Handsome? Wonderful?"

"More like aggravating." I stormed back down the hallway and locked the bedroom door behind me.

Chapter Nine: Safe in My Castle

"Merry!" squealed the tiny blonde human behind the Brooks' giant door.

"Hi, pretty girl!" I wrapped my arm around her.

Chase trotted down the spiral stairs. "Good morning, sunshine."

"Where are you going?" Khloe asked.

"To work." He kissed the top of her head. "See ya later, squirt."

"Oh." Her shoulders slumped. "I thought Merry was staying."

"You have to go to school. But what do you say we go to dinner later?"

"With Merry?"

They both looked at me.

"Sure. I'll come."

Khloe jumped up and down excitedly. "Have a good day at work! See you later!"

Chase closed the door behind us as we walked out to his car.

"So, are you still mad at me?"

"For breaking into my apartment?"

"I didn't break in. Shelly let me in. And I didn't know you were in the shower."

"Yeah, yeah. A likely story."

Chase sat back in his seat and smiled. "Last day with your sling."

I sighed. "I know. Too bad I don't have a car to drive now."

"I'm sorry." He patted his steering wheel. "You can borrow mine any time you want."

"Really?"

"Of course. Why not?"

"I didn't think you allowed anyone to drive it."

"I don't allow just anyone to drive it."

"I just miss it. Driving was always an escape for me. After my mom left, I would wait until my dad was asleep, and I would get in my car and go."

"Where would you go?"

"Anywhere. Nowhere. There is something so exhilarating about driving in the dark, without anyone on the road, completely aimless. It's like my endorphins would kick in, and could override any pain or sadness I was experiencing."

"That's how I feel when I'm on stage."

As we pulled up to the shop, I noticed it was open already. "How is it open if your parents are at home?"

Chase sighed. "Tanner has been opening early to get a head start on things. My dad has been going to a lot of doctor's appointments lately. Tanner hasn't been dealing well with everything. I think he comes here just to keep his mind busy."

"And how are you dealing with everything?"

He shut the engine and we sat in the parking lot for a few minutes. His eyebrows pushed together, as he ran his fingers through his hair. "I don't know, honestly. I try not to think about it, but my mind keeps arriving at exactly that one thing I don't want to think about." He looked up at me. "I'm glad you'll be here working with me."

"Me, too."

Inside, Tanner was working under a car with his headphones on. I wondered how long he had been here.

Chase walked me over to a car that was already up on the lift. "My dad left a list of cars that need their brakes done. Brake pads are over here. All the tools you'll need are here."

I nodded as he pointed. "What do I work on when I'm finished with these?"

"Don't get ahead of yourself," Tanner called from where he was working. "Just focus on the list."

Chase opened his mouth to respond, but I held my hand up to stop him. I walked over to where Tanner was now standing. "I just wanted to know what else I should be doing. This way, I don't have to keep bothering you every five minutes, asking what I should do next. You guys need help, and I'm here to do that. Simple."

"Get through the list first, and we'll see how much of a help you are." He abruptly sat and rolled back under the car.

I looked at Chase, who was clenching his jaw from where he stood, and overdramatically rolled my eyes. His mouth slowly turned up into a smile.

"Get to work," I growled as I swiped the list out of his hands.

His smile turned into a grin as he walked away.

It felt good to be busy working in a garage again – too good to let anything else bother me. It passed the time and kept my mind occupied. I felt productive. Everything else in the world was shut out by the sounds of air compressors and metal clanking.

It was also thoroughly enjoyable watching Chase work. The focused expression on his face was incredibly sexy, while the muscles in his arms stretched and pulled with every twist and jerk. I had to face the opposite direction after I felt the schoolgirl smile plastered on my face. I hoped Tanner did not notice.

By the end of the day, I had completed the list of relatively small jobs Tim had left. I also did several oil changes and tune ups. Every now and again, I noticed Tanner sneaking a peek at me. He said nothing each time, and I was glad. The less we talked, the better. I did not like seeing the brothers at odds, and definitely did not want to upset Tanner any more than he already was.

At five o'clock, Chase took out his keys after cleaning up his area. "You ready?"

I nodded. "Just need to put these away. You go. I'll be out there in a minute."

He glanced at Tanner before walking into the front office.

I put all of the tools back in their respective drawers, and grabbed my purse.

Tanner looked up as I walked over to him. He took out one of his earbuds. "You did good work today."

His compliment took me by surprise, though I would not let him see it. "We're taking Khloe to dinner. You should come."

He shook his head, and looked down at his hands. "Nah."

I took a deep breath and spoke gently. "Isolating yourself from your family will only make it worse."

He looked up again, this time with fire in his eyes. "Your dad dies and you're a shrink now?"

I took the bullet. I expected it. "Yeah, but lucky for you this first consultation is free."

"Well, I don't need advice from anyone. Especially not you."

"You're right. You don't need advice. It doesn't matter what anyone else thinks you should do, or how you should feel. If you're angry, feel angry. If you're sad, feel sad. Scream, cry, throw things – do whatever you need to do to get it out. But don't do it alone. Your family needs you, and you need them. Just because your dad is dying doesn't mean you get to act like a dick. The rest of your family is still alive. They're going through the same thing you are – they don't deserve your bitterness and anger. It's not their fault. They're all suffering right along with you. Your mom and dad, most of all. Imagine how your mom feels, having to watch her children grieve the loss of their parent. And your dad – he knows he's leaving his family behind, and there's nothing he can do to stop it. You need to cherish these last moments with each other, and stop wasting your time taking your anger out on the wrong people. You can make your comments at me, I don't care. Life sucks sometimes, I know. It fucks us all in different ways. But you and your brother should be picking up the pieces together. Don't do this alone – and don't make him go through this alone, either."

I watched as he forced the welling tears to remain behind his lids that were about to brim over – something I was very familiar with. We stood there in silence, until I accepted the fact that silence was all there would be at this point.

"Want us to bring you back anything?" I tried one final attempt.

"No thanks." He put his earbud back in and slid under the car.

"What took you so long?" Chase asked when I finally sat in the passenger seat next to him.

"I just wanted to clean my area. I've only got one arm, you know."

"You didn't let that stop you today. You even left Tanner speechless. He's never speechless."

"Cut him some slack. He's going through a lot right now."

"We're all going through a lot right now. That doesn't give him the right to treat people badly."

"I know. But everybody goes through things differently. Right now, he's angry."

"So you're saying I should ignore his asshole comments?"

"You ignore most of mine, don't you?"

His eyes softened.

"We take things out on the ones closest to us. It's easy because we know they will always be there, and forgive us. He's angry, so let him be angry."

When he pulled into his driveway, Khloe came running outside before the car was in park. She ferociously waved with one hand, while holding her car seat in the other. I couldn't help but chuckle.

Chase clipped her in behind me, and we were on our way.

"Where are we going?" she asked excitedly.

"Let's do the diner," Chase suggested. "You can have breakfast for dinner, if you'd like."

Her squeal sounded through the car. "Yay! Pancakes!"

"My favorite," I cheered along with her.

"Merry, do you like puppies?"

"Yes, I love puppies. Do you?"

"Yup. Mommy said I can get a puppy one day."

"What kind of puppy would you want?"

"The kind that gets really big when he grows up." She held her hands out on either side of her to show me just how big she wants her puppy to be.

"Ooh, I love big dogs."

"Why don't you get one, too?" she inquired.

"I'm not ready to take care of a pet, yet. I can just about take care of a pet rock right now."

"A pet rock?!" The car filled with her high-pitched giggle again. "That's silly, Merry."

"What will you name your puppy when you get him?"

"I don't know. I can't think of any names I like." She sounded disappointed.

"That's okay. You have to meet him first, to see his personality. Then the perfect name will come to you."

"Then you can come over and play with him. We can take him on walks, and feed him, and teach him tricks."

"And pick up his poop all over the yard," Chase chimed in.

She scrunched up her nose. "Ew! I don't want to touch his poop!"

"That can be Chase's job. He can be the pooper scooper upper."

Her laughter was a beautiful sound.

"She thinks you're hysterical." Chase was grinning from ear to ear, watching her in the rearview mirror.

When we got out of the car, Khloe held my hand as we walked in the parking lot. Inside, she let go and followed the hostess to our table, skipping happily ahead of us. When we reached our booth, she pulled me in beside her. "Sit next to me, Merry!"

"I've been replaced." Chase clutched his heart as he slumped over in the booth.

"They have the best apple pie here." I pointed to the desserts on Khloe's menu.

"Ooh, can we get apple pie, Chasey?" She bounced up and down excitedly.

"Yeah, Chasey-poo. Can we?" I teased.

"If you both eat your dinner, we'll talk about it."

Khloe nodded as she began coloring the picture on her placemat. I watched her as she worked, her sweet eyes so big and focused. Everything on her was perfect. Her little round nostrils, her soft cheeks, her puffy pink lips. I reached out to stroke her golden hair.

"Merry," she started, without looking up from her coloring. "Are you and Chase going to get married?"

Chase nearly choked on the water he was sipping.

"Why do you ask?"

"If you marry Chase, you'd be like my big sister. Then you'd be in our family forever, and I could see you all the time."

"You can see me whenever you want. We don't have to be married for that."

"But I really love you. And I know Chase loves you, too."

"How do you know that?" Chase intercepted.

"I know that when you love someone, you take care of them all the time. You always want to be around them, because they make your heart happy." She stopped coloring to look at him. "Doesn't Merry make your heart happy?"

"She does."

"And does Chase make your heart happy?" Both Khloe and Chase looked at me with the same exact eyes.

"He does." I took her hand and placed it inside of mine. "And so do you. You make my heart very, very happy."

She smiled, satisfied with our answers, and went back to coloring.

"Speaking of marriage, where are your parents tonight?" I asked Chase.

"They went out. They do date night once a week now."

"That's sweet."

"It is. I can only hope my marriage is like theirs one day."

"Chase Brooks wants to get married?"

"Sure. Don't you?"

I shrugged. "I never really thought about what it would be like if and when I got married, or if I'd ever have children. Taking care of my dad as much as I did, my prospects didn't look too hopeful."

"Well, things are pretty different for you now."

"I know. We'll see, I guess."

"I want to be the flower girl!" Khloe exclaimed.

I imagined how beautiful she would look with a puffy white dress on, and pink flowers in her wavy hair. She wouldn't be one of those kids who was too shy to walk down the aisle on her own. My mind then wandered to imagine Chase in a perfectly-tailored tux, his hair flawlessly coiffed, and smiling his brilliant smile. I wondered what the girl who got to marry Chase Brooks would be like; I wondered if I would like her; I wondered if Khloe would like her; I wondered if he and I would remain friends. Shelly's question suddenly entered my mind: What happens if he gets a girlfriend? What will you feel like then?

"You ok?" Chase asked when our pancakes arrived.

I nodded and smiled, trying to push the thoughts out of my head.

Khloe jumped from topic to topic while shoving forkfuls of pancakes into her overly stuffed mouth. I loved conversations with her. They were so genuine. She held nothing back – kids never have filters. They spew from the brain, always saying exactly what they think. Sometimes I wished I could do the same. She talked until she passed out in the back seat of Chase's car on the ride home.

I snuck a peek at her over my shoulder.

"You sure you're okay?" Chase asked in a low voice.

"Yeah. Why do you keep asking?"

"You just seem… far away. Does it have anything to do with why you were crying with Shelly yesterday?"

I rested my head back on the seat. "I'm just tired. It's been a long day."

"You have a big day ahead of you tomorrow. Finally getting your sling off. How do you feel?"

"Relieved. It's finally over. No more depending on people to do everything for me."

"It hasn't been that terrible, has it?"

I looked at him with a confused expression. "My sling?"

"I mean, I know you hate depending on people to do things for you. But it hasn't been that bad, with me driving you around and helping you out. Right?"

I turned in my seat to face him. "It has not been bad at all. You have helped me in more ways than I can count. I appreciate you so much."

He pulled into his driveway and turned the engine off. "I've been wondering if you won't want me around anymore."

"Why would you even think that?"

He shrugged. "You won't need me."

"Chase, I don't hang around you because I need you to help me. I enjoy your company. I like spending time with you. You think I hang out with you because I have to? Have you thought this the entire time?" I searched his eyes for an answer while I waited for his response.

"I don't really know what to think… you're not exactly forthcoming with your thoughts and feelings. You keep everything locked up inside like a castle."

I laughed.

"And now you're laughing at me…"

"No, no. I'm not laughing at you! Shelly told me something yesterday, and it reminded me of what you just said."

"Oh, yeah? What was that?"

"She told me that I'm a warrior. She called me Xena."

He grinned. "The warrior princess. You totally are."

"I know I'm difficult. I know I keep my feelings to myself. But all my life, I've been on my own. I take care of myself, and I don't let people in because it's easier. I don't know how to be any other way."

"Things are going to get better for you."

"And how do you know this?"

"Because I happen to know that people don't always hurt you."

"I'll believe it when I see it."

His eyes looked straight into mine. "I will never hurt you."

I foolishly held his stare, allowing myself to dive head first into the depth of his eyes. It was easy to believe them. They looked into your soul, and could convince you of anything.

"You believe me, don't you?" He lifted his hand and brushed his fingertips against my cheek.

I allowed him to linger there, as my skin tingled under touch. "I want to."

"I promise you, I will always take care of you. I-"

"Where are we?" A sleepy Khloe sat up in her car seat. She rubbed her eye with a tiny fist. "Are we home?"

"Yes, we're home. I'll carry you up to bed." Chase looked at me. "Will you stay? I'll only be a few minutes."

"I think I'm going to call it a night." I felt terrible bailing on him in the middle of our conversation, but I just wasn't ready. "I'll see you tomorrow, though."

"Okay. Goodnight."

"Night." I got out of the car, and leaned into the back seat to give Khloe a quick hug. "Goodnight, little nugget."

"Bye, Merry," she replied sleepily.

I watched as Chase carried her up the driveway to the front door, her little hands clutching his shoulders. Part of me wanted to run after him, to tell him that I wanted to hear all that he wanted to say. Instead, I walked up the concrete steps to my apartment and locked the door behind me. Safe in my castle.

Chapter Ten: Halloween

"Pearls or choker?" Shelly held up two different necklaces. She wore a black sequined headband around her forehead to match her black shimmery flapper dress. Her red hair was tucked underneath her blonde pin-curled wig. She looked flawless.

"You should definitely go with the pearls," I decided.

"Good. This choker will go great with your dress!"

It made me happy to see her so excited about her birthday party. With my wild hair under the black wig, I looked like a different person. My dress was one-shouldered, hiding the surgery scars perfectly. It was a tad shorter than I had wanted, but the silver fringe sparkled as it moved. I slipped my silver heels on while Shelly fastened the string of faux diamonds around my neck.

"We look fabulous!" she squealed. She unlocked my bedroom door, and walked out.

Admittedly, I was eager to see how Chase looked as a 1920's gangster. When we stepped into the living room, he was sitting on the arm of the couch with his black hat dipped over one eye. His pinstriped vest was buttoned tightly around his midsection with a white tie tucked into it, and his black dress shirt sleeves were rolled up to his elbows. He looked incredibly sexy.

We had not spoken about our interrupted conversation all week. He was undoubtedly waiting to see if I would bring it up, while I was hoping he wouldn't.

His grin spread from ear to ear when he saw me. "Lookin' good, doll face."

I pulled at my dress nervously. "Thanks. It's a little short."

"Stop trying to pull it down! Show off those legs! Let's go. I can't wait to see Brody!" Shelly practically dragged me out the door and down the stairs to Chase's car.

The party was in full effect when we arrived. Music could be heard from down the street as we turned the corner to park. Fake webbing decorated the bushes and trees outside the Beta house. Orange string lights wrapped around the railing leading to the entryway. Chase pushed open the door, and the blaring music instantly hit us.

As expected, there were sexy variations of every profession walking around with their cleavage exposed. Skeletons, zombies, and ghosts hung on every wall. A space was cleared near the back for the dance floor, where an orange and black disco ball hung from the ceiling. The usual birthday banner hung from the wall in honor of Shelly. One of the frat brothers stood behind the DJ booth with one ear in his headphones.

"You guys look amazing!" Kenzie cried as she rushed up to us in full Batgirl costume.

"You, too! Have you seen Brody anywhere?" Shelly's eyes searched the first floor.

"I'll go find him." Chase disappeared up the stairs.

Tina stood from a nearby couch. She was in a red leotard with red horns sticking up out of her hair.

"Where's your costume?" I asked, poking her pitchfork.

"Very funny. I haven't heard that one yet."

"How has it been working at the shop?" Kenzie inquired.

"It's great. I'm finally doing something besides sitting in the house."

"So, are you just done with school now? Are you dropping out for good?" Tina was never one to beat around the bush.

"I don't know. I'm taking it one day at a time right now."

"You can still work and go to school at the same time."

"Yeah, right," Shelly interjected. "She's been working all day, every day!"

"I bet she is." Tina gestured to Chase as he came down the stairs, with Brody in tow.

"I haven't figured everything out, yet. I'll let you know when I do." I didn't know how to explain the hours I had been working without spilling Chase's secret. His father's health was on a steady decline, and the Brooks brothers were determined to keep everything up and running in Tim's absence.

Shelly ran to Brody and jumped into his arms.

"Happy birthday, gorgeous!"

"It looks great in here," she exclaimed, looking around. "Let's get everybody drinks." She grabbed Brody's arm with one hand, my wrist with her other, and pulled us into the kitchen.

"If you keep pulling on me like this, I'm going to need surgery on my other shoulder."

"Here, hold this." She pulled a tray out of the refrigerator and handed it to me.

I peered into the small gelatin cups as I placed them down onto the counter. As Kenzie and Tina entered behind us, Shelly handed them a shot. She gestured to Brody and Chase. Brody knew better than to argue, and took the shot.

"No shots for me." Chase held his hands up. "I'm good with beer." He reached into a cooler nearby and took a beer out. He reached in again and handed me a water bottle. I hid behind him and poured the water into an orange cup while Shelly threw back two shots.

"Why are you crouching behind me?" he asked.

"Shelly will be getting very drunk tonight. I will be holding a cup to give her the illusion I am drinking with her."

He chuckled. "Very clever."

"I don't want anything spoiling her fun – especially not me."

"Well, you'd better get out there then." He gestured to the next room.

Shelly was already dancing in her favorite spot in the middle of the dance floor. We all danced around her, belting out the lyrics of each song that came on. Without even realizing it, I was having a blast, too. I was glad the sling came off in time for the party. It was a constant visual representation of weakness – of all the ways my life had been debilitated. Though my shoulder wasn't fully healed yet, it felt good to have my arm free.

Several songs in and an unknown amount of alcohol later, Shelly, the Selfie Queen, was in full effect. We took countless combinations of photos until my cheeks hurt from smiling.

"No more!" I shouted to her.

"Just one more," she insisted. "You need to take one with Chase. For your frame!"

I pressed my cheek against his as he wrapped his arms around me. I held onto his midsection and tried to steady the both of us. I didn't know how many beers he had consumed, but he seemed a bit wobbly.

"You guys look adorable!" Shelly squealed and she captured the moment on her phone.

Chase scooped me up and twirled me in a circle before setting me down. The song changed, and I stared up into his eyes as our bodies began to move in time with the beat.

"You owe me a dance."

I smirked, well aware that he would not forget my promise from when I was still in the sling. "Don't let this go to your head or anything, but you look really great tonight."

His face lit up when he smiled. "So do you. I miss your curls, though."

I scrunched my nose up. "Why?"

"It's you."

"A big hot mess?"

"Stunningly beautiful."

I turned around to avoid getting hypnotized by his gaze, pressing my back up against him. His hands gripped my waist and I could feel his breath on my neck. The voice in my head that was screaming for me to stop now became a faint whisper. Dancing wrapped up in Chase's arms felt too good to ignore. The lines that I had so carefully drawn around our friendship were blurring. What was once crystal clear, black and white, had just turned into foggy grey confusion.

He spun me around to face him again, pulling me close to his body so that the space between us disappeared. I could hardly hear the music as he ran his hands down my back. The trance we were in made it feel like we were the only two people on the dance floor. We were barely moving anymore, as he took my face into his hands. Our lips were inches away, and without hesitation I stretched up onto my toes to get closer to his mouth.

Our lips were about to touch when a drunken sexy firewoman knocked into us before crashing onto the floor. Her drink spilled down my arm, soaking one side of my dress. It felt like I was being woken up with a cold splash of water, and just like that – the spell between Chase and I had been broken. I stepped back in realization of what was just about to happen, and quickly escaped to the kitchen. Shelly was hot on my heels.

"Are you okay?"

"I'm fine, just wet."

She took the entire roll of paper towels off the holder and started dabbing at my dress.

"Don't worry about the dress." I tore a few cloths off the roll and dried my arm.

"What the hell was going on?" She drunkenly exclaimed. "Did you kiss him?"

"No! I don't know what I was doing!" My entire body was tingling, and I couldn't tell if it was from Chase or the cold drink.

She picked up a shot and handed it to me. "You could use this right now."

"I can't. I'm pretty sure Chase won't be able to drive home."

She pouted. "I don't want to drink alone."

"You're not." I waved my arm around the room. "Everyone here is wasted right along with you."

"I'm not wasted. You're wasted."

I giggled and gave her a nudge. "Go."

The boys were now at the pool table a few feet from the dance floor. I let out a sigh of relief that I did not have to dance with Chase again. I don't know what had come over me, but I was afraid it would happen again if he came any closer.

As the night continued, Shelly and Chase were sporting similar looks: eyes half closed, teetering from one side to the other. It was Kenzie's turn to be on Shelly duty. Tina and I sat on the couch laughing and making fun of them.

I stifled a yawn.

"Are you ready for bed, old lady?" Tina teased.

"It's been a while since I've been out like this. I forgot how exhausting it is."

"Well, it's nice to have you back." She motioned to Chase at the pool table. "What's new with him?"

I shrugged. "Same as the last time I saw you."

"You're still going to play the friend card, huh?"

"I don't know what else to tell you, Tee."

"You're too dark for him, you know."

"I'm not dark."

"You have been through shit. You're tough, you're sarcastic, and cynical. What could you possibly see in a two-dimensional preppy boy like Chase?"

"He's not two-dimensional. There's more to him than you would think."

"More to him than sex and muscles?"

"He's a good person, with a good heart. He's smart, he's funny. The muscles are just a plus."

"Caring, intelligent, sense of humor, delicious body... he sounds like he's the perfect man."

"He is."

"So, let me get this straight: you've found the perfect man; he's interested in you; but you keep telling him that you're just friends?"

"Well, it sounds bad when you put it like that."

Tina shook her head. "It sounds crazy. Maybe you bumped your head a little harder than we all thought in that accident. You might be missing a few screws up there."

"You always know how to make me feel good."

She smirked as she put her arm around me. "If I were you, that's the Brooks brother I'd be after." She pointed at Tanner, who was playing pool at a table just beyond Chase.

"You like Tanner?"

"I like the thought of Tanner on me."

"You two would be great. He's an asshole, you're an asshole. It would be a match made in hell."

Tina laughed. "Come on. Let's go rescue Kenzie."

Shelly threw her arms around me when I got onto the dance floor. "Let's do another shot," she slurred into my ear.

"You're done doing shots."

"Will you dance with me?"

I laughed. "I am dancing with you."

Suddenly, I felt two hands take my hips and pull me backwards. I looked over my shoulder, expecting to see Chase. Instead, it was Shawn, wearing his impish smile as he tried to grind against me. I pushed him away, but he recovered quickly and pulled aggressively on my arm to get closer. I let out a yelp in pain. He reeked of beer and body odor.

"Let go of me!"

Tina tried pulling him off, but he only held on tighter. I saw her eyes widen as she looked past me, and then she backed away from us.

Tanner appeared out of nowhere, and gripped two handfuls of Shawn's shirt in his fists.

"She doesn't want to dance, bro." He glared down at Shawn

with a scary look in his eyes. I was relieved when Shawn raised his hands to surrender.

"It's okay, Tanner," I shouted over the music. If he ended up with a broken hand, Chase and I would be completely backed up at work.

When Tanner loosened his grip, Shawn leaned in and whispered something into his ear. Without even winding up to swing, Tanner's huge fist smashed into Shawn's nose. Blood spewed out all over the floor, and my hands flew up to my mouth in horror. Shawn fell instantly. Everybody in the room crowded around the two of them.

I grabbed Shelly's elbow and pulled her towards the pool tables.

"Where are you taking me?" she whined.

"It's time to go."

Brody met us before we reached Chase. He took Shelly from me and guided us through the crowd. "Grab him," he shouted in my ear as we passed Chase.

I reached out and took Chase's hand while Brody steadily pushed me out the door, and down the stairs.

Finally, we arrived next to Chase's car.

"Okay, okay. You can stop pushing me. We're safe."

"Sorry, I had to get you guys out of there." Brody steadied Shelly and reached into his pocket for his keys.

I rubbed my back where he was pushing me. "Thanks. I'll think of you when I'm pissing blood tomorrow."

Chase and Shelly both burst out laughing, swaying in the street.

"Isn't she so funny?" Chase asked.

"She's the funniest," Shelly answered in the same slow tone.

"Are you able to get him home?" Brody asked, ignoring the pair of idiots that stood beside us.

I nodded. "We're both going to the same house. I'll take him. Just put her hair up before she starts puking."

"You got it." He gestured to Chase, who was now peeing in the middle of the street. "Good luck with that."

I groaned and covered my eyes. I waited until I heard the zipper on his pants and it was safe to look. "Where are your keys?"

Chase shrugged and leaned over the trunk of his car.

I sighed and reached into his pants pockets. He laughed and twitched. "That tickles."

"Hold still before I grab the wrong thing. You won't be laughing then."

He only laughed harder.

When I finally found his keys, I opened the passenger door and tried to guide him into the seat. It was like trying to herd a giant bee into a keyhole.

"Watch your head. Watch your head. Okay, there you go." As I belted him, I felt a smile creeping across my face.

"Why are you smiling?" He slurred.

"I get my sling off and now I'm the one clipping you into your seat."

He grinned his perfect grin, his teeth gleaming under the streetlight. His head fell back on the headrest.

I hopped into the driver's seat and turned the ignition. It felt so good to be behind the wheel again – especially one of such an awesome vehicle. I tore the itchy wig off my head, tossed it into the back seat, and shook out my hair. I adjusted the seat and mirrors, and ran my hands over the steering wheel while I revved the engine. I rolled my window all the way down before driving away. This was the moment I had been waiting for. I could feel my cheeks pushing up as the smile spread out across my face.

"You look so hot driving my car," Chase mumbled. He leaned over and tried to caress my face.

I swatted him away. "Watch my eyes."

I thundered down the road, the dead leaves on the street whirling up around the car. The roar of the engine as we flew by was a tranquil sound. It was the first moment in a very long time that my mind was clear, as if all of my worries were left behind. Though the ride home was short, I enjoyed every second of it.

When we pulled up, it was after one o'clock in the morning. I killed the engine and took a deep breath. I did not know how I planned on getting Chase up the stairs. I walked around to his side, and pulled as hard as I could to get him up and out of the car.

"I'm heavy."

"Yeah, no shit," I grunted. He leaned on me as I tried to walk him up the driveway. "You could help me out a little."

"Where are you taking me?" he asked.

"I'm taking you to sleep on my couch. You can't go in your house like this and wake everybody up."

"We're having a sleepover?"

"Yes, if we ever make it up these stairs. Step. Okay next step." I guided his legs up each concrete step. "You have to lift your leg!"

"I know how stairs work," he slurred.

"Well, it's not looking that way at the moment. Come on, one more. There you go." I propped him against the railing while I unlocked my door and caught my breath. I directed him into the living room and gave him a push when we neared the couch. He fell like a tree and bounced onto the cushions. I could no longer contain my laughter.

"Why are you laughing at me?"

"You would be laughing if you saw yourself right now." I untied his shoelaces, and slid off each shoe. "Sit up. Let me take this vest off."

He sat up with his eyes closed. "I always knew you wanted to undress me."

"Shut up, or I won't help your drunk ass."

His eyes opened while I yanked off his vest and began unbuttoning his shirt. He played with a strand of my hair. I let him. It kept him still. His hand then moved to my cheek, and he began tracing my bottom lip with his thumb. His touch caused a warm sensation to spread throughout my body.

"Chase," I warned.

"I want to kiss you."

"I don't."

His hand dropped immediately. "You don't?"

"Not when you're like this, I don't."

"You almost kissed me before."

"I don't know what happened."

"Yes, you do! You wanted to kiss me, too."

"Well, I don't want to kiss you now. You're drunk. You won't even remember any of this in the morning."

"Yes I will. Just say it. Admit it."

I tugged on his sleeves and pulled them off, revealing his bare torso right before my eyes. His skin looked smooth, and it took all of my restraint to not reach out and touch him. I debated whether or not to take off his pants. Sleeping in jeans would not be comfortable, but he would be in a drunken coma, so it probably would not matter. Though we had grown close over the past month, he had not divulged whether he was a boxers, briefs, or commando kind of guy – I didn't need any surprises tonight.

"Lay down. I'll get you a blanket."

His shoulders dropped and he flopped backwards onto the couch. I knew he was frustrated with me, but luckily the alcohol coursing through his veins would help put him to sleep quickly.

I returned with the throw blanket that was atop my comforter. I spread the blanket over his body and knelt beside him. "Comfortable?"

His eyes were closed again. "I'd be more comfortable if you were lying here with me."

"I'll be right in the next room. Do you think you'll need a garbage pail?"

"No. I don't puke." He reached for my hand and interlocked his fingers with mine. "Why won't you let me in?"

"I did let you in. You're lying on my couch." I lifted his hand and tucked it under the blanket.

He opened his eyes. Though they were glassy, they focused precisely on mine. "You know what I mean, Merr."

Even while he was intoxicated, his stare drew me in. I ran my fingers through his hair in spite of myself. "Everything is finally good – it's really good. I don't want anything to screw that up."

"Everything is so good because we are together. Don't you see that?" His eyes slowly began to close.

I rubbed his head until he fell asleep, which did not take long. His lips slightly parted and he was breathing deeply. I lingered a moment, watching him sleep.

Chase was right; everything was better ever since he came into my life. I could feel the barrier I had built long ago start to weaken. The more time I spent with him, the harder he became to resist. Was resisting the right thing to do? I had once thought so. Now, I was unsure. I was certain of one thing, though: one kiss would change everything.

Chapter Eleven: The Box

"Help!" I screamed. The flames roared around me. I could barely breathe in the smoke-filled car. My left arm would not move; it felt like something was crushing it. I pulled harder, but it only made the stabbing pain worse. The heat was unbearable. Red liquid was streaming into my eyes, making it harder to see. I was trapped. I tried to call for help again, but no sound came out. I choked on the thick black smoke. I let the realization sink in: I was going to die.

I looked one last time out the window. That's when I saw it. A dark figure, not too far from my mangled car, was approaching. I squinted through the blood and the smoke, but couldn't make out who or what the figure was. I could hear my name being called. It sounded so close. I closed my eyes.

"Merritt! You have to wake up!"

I opened my eyes, and Chase was standing over me. I was in my yellow bedroom, drenched in sweat. The sun was shining through the windows onto my bed. I sat up and rubbed my eyes.

"Are you okay?" He sat on the edge of the bed, a troubled look on his face.

I nodded, trying to catch my breath.

"Was it the dream?"

I nodded again. "Was I screaming?"

"I heard a sound coming from your room. When I checked on you, you were crying. I figured you'd want to be woken up."

"It was so weird. The dream was… it was different this time."

He raised his eyebrows. "How so?"

"At the end, right before I was supposed to die, I saw something."

"Something?"

"Or someone. I don't know. I couldn't see it clearly. It was a figure, coming towards me."

"And that never happened in any of your other dreams?"

"No. This was the first time."

"Maybe all the Halloween decorations from last night stuck in your mind, or something."

Last night. The party. Chase was drunk. "Oh. How are you feeling?" I let my gaze lower to his bare upper body. "You look better than I thought you would."

He grinned. "I'm fine. Just drank one too many beers."

"I'm glad you didn't blow chunks on my new carpet."

"I told you, I don't puke."

"Oh, so you remember telling me that?"

"Of course. I remember everything."

I felt a twinge in my stomach. "I should probably see how Shelly's doing. And take a shower."

He stood, but lingered. "Thanks for taking care of me last night."

I waved my hand. "Please. You've taken care of me enough times. I didn't mind."

He stepped towards the door, but then turned back around. "Maybe we can finish that conversation sometime. The one we had last night."

"Sure."

After a pause, he walked out of the room to grab his things.

I waited until I heard the front door close before I hopped out of bed and into the shower.

For the remainder of the morning, I relaxed on the recliner watching movies, waiting for Shelly to wake up. My mind frequently wandered back to dancing with Chase the night before. His lips were so close, it would have been easy to have kissed them. I wondered how differently this morning would have gone if I had.

A knock at my door in the late afternoon pulled me out of my thoughts.

"Look away!" Shelly shouted, as I swung open the door. Hiding her face in the crook of her elbow, she walked past me and continued her dramatics as she threw herself onto the couch.

I closed the door, chuckling to myself.

"I can hear you laughing at me!"

"If you opened your eyes, you could see me laughing at you, too."

"I think I threw up my spleen around three-thirty."

"Fun night, huh?"

"I only remember it in fragments," she groaned.

"Most people consider that a great night."

"Please tell me you're coming to dinner. If my parents ask me one more time how you're doing, my head might explode."

"I'll be there."

"What's wrong? You seem distracted or something."

"Something happened. Something weird."

"Between you and Chase?!" She sat up, instantly feeling better.

"No, no. Let me finish. I had my nightmare again… but this time, at the end, there was a black figure walking towards the car."

"What happened?"

"Nothing. Chase woke me up. He said he heard me crying."

"Wait – Chase was here?"

"He slept on the couch. Focus, Shell."

"Sorry. Okay, so you saw someone coming towards you. Maybe it's the person who pulled you out of your car. Maybe your brain is remembering more. The doctor said you might gain some memories back from the night of your accident over time."

I shrugged. "I don't know. Why now, all of a sudden?"

"Why are you so opposed to finding out who it was? I would be dying to know!"

"If the person wanted to be recognized for it, he would have come forward by now. I respect the fact that the person wants privacy."

"Maybe he's shy. Or she. What if it's a she?"

"You're obsessed, dude."

"Yeah, I am obsessed with the person who saved my best friend's life. He deserves all the thanks in the fucking world, if you ask me."

"I'm sorry. You have every right to be curious. It just doesn't really matter to me."

"You know what I really want to know? What it felt like dancing with Chase Brooks last night."

Now it was my turn to hide my face in shame. "I don't want to talk about it!"

"I'm going to put that on your tombstone, I swear. Here lies Merritt Adams. Beloved daughter and friend. She doesn't want to talk about it!"

"There's nothing to talk about. I got caught up in a moment of weakness. There was something in the air – it was the Halloween air!

"Or love is in the air," she cooed.

"No. It most definitely did not smell like love!"

"I think it smells exactly like love. And do you want to know what else I think?"

"No, but you're going to tell me anyway."

"The doctor told you that the more you hold onto feelings of anger and sadness, the longer it will take your brain to recover any lost memories. If you are a closed-off person, your brain becomes closed off, too. You are trying so hard to ignore any feelings you have for Chase, and remain closed off, that you're shutting out the memories that want to come back, too."

"So, you're saying if I admit that I have feelings for Chase, that my memory of the accident will miraculously come back?"

"Not when you put it like that." She sighed. "I just mean that you need to open up more about your feelings in life. Be more open."

"I can do that."

She raised her eyebrows. "Really?"

"Sure. Right now, I am feeling very hungry. I'd like to leave so we can go to your parents' house. There – how was that for expressing my feelings?"

She hurled a pillow at me and stood. "You're such a bitch."

I chuckled as I followed her down the stairs to her car.

"Laugh all you want. You don't fool me. I've got your number. You don't have to admit it, but I know you're falling in love with him."

"Falling in love with who?" a deep voice behind us asked.

I whirled around to see Tanner walking down his driveway. "Nobody," I replied quickly. "How's your hand?"

He shrugged as he shoved his swollen knuckles into his pocket. "It's fine. Better than Shawn's face."

"Can I ask why you punched him? What did he say to you?"

"He said that if I wasn't going to fuck you, someone else would."

I shuddered at the thought. "He's such a skeeze ball."

"Yup."

"Well, thanks."

"For what?"

"For getting him off of me."

He nodded and got into his car. He backed out of the driveway, and stopped when he reached me in front of Shelly's car by the curb. "Hey, Merritt."

"Yeah?"

"Don't break my brother's heart."

I was stunned that Tanner even cared about his brother's feelings. "I wouldn't do that."

He rolled up his window and sped down the block.

I got into the passenger seat beside Shelly.

"You see? Even he knows you're in love with Chase."

I shot her a look, and turned on the radio so we could drive the entire way to New Jersey without talking.

When we were in kindergarten, Shelly's mother was pregnant with another daughter. She ended up having a miscarriage. Shelly always said that I was like the sister she never got to have, and her parents treated me as such. Growing up, Shelly's parents – Betty and Don – always seemed perfect: they acted like Shelly's friends, and had a great, honest relationship with her. The revelation of Don's secret five-year gambling problem almost tore the family apart. They lost almost everything, and had to move where it was cheaper in south New Jersey. Since Shelly was already in her freshman year of college, she got her own apartment and opted to stay in Staten Island. Don went to rehab, and they were still able to live happily ever after.

It was strange pulling up to their mobile home, though I had been there many times before. I had not seen them since the day I left the hospital after waking up from the coma. I secretly was not looking forward to this dinner – anyone who hadn't seen me since the accident always poked and prodded with the same questions. It was like a broken record that I could not stop. I put on my game face as I stepped through the door of their mobile home.

"My girls are home!" Betty shouted. She threw her arms around the both of us and crushed us in her embrace.

"Ma! Watch Merr's shoulder!"

"Oh! Oh! I'm so sorry. Are you okay?"

I laughed. "I'm fine. How are you? You look great!"

"I'm down ten pounds since the last time you saw me." She faced sideways, showing off her slimmer waistline.

"Wow, mom. Look at you! What are you trying to find a boyfriend?"

"Yeah," Don called from the kitchen. "One with more hair!"

"Maybe we should hire a pool boy," Betty called back to him.

Shelly shook her head. "Oh, you have a pool now?"

"You don't need a pool to get a pool boy." Betty winked at me.

"Ew," Shelly grimaced. "Enough of this. I actually want to have an appetite for dinner."

I followed the smell of Shelly's favorite dinner – chicken parmigiana with spaghetti – into the tiny kitchen. "Smells great in here, Don."

Don turned around, in his Kiss the Cook apron, and opened his arms. "Get over here, kid."

Our hug lingered as I closed my eyes and took in the familiarity all around me. The smell of a home cooked meal; the sound of football on the television in the next room; the feeling of being home with family.

"Alright, alright," Shelly interrupted. "Your second favorite daughter is here now." She always joked that Don favored me. Truthfully, I think he just felt guilty about blowing all of his money and not being able to help me through my financial hardship with my father. So, he overcompensated with love.

Don chuckled. "Shut up and hug me."

"Hi Dad."

"Hi, my baby. Go sit. Dinner's ready."

We walked over to the kitchen table that was already set.

"You didn't have to break out the fine China for us," Shelly teased, picking up the paper plate in front of her.

"Shut up!" I whispered.

"With the easy cleanup, you don't have to help with the dishes later," Betty stated matter-of-factly. "You're welcome."

I laughed. "Nice, Betty."

We sat while Don brought out a heaping bowl of spaghetti. "Mangia!" he shouted in Italian, gesturing for us to dig in.

I giggled. "I miss hearing that."

"Now that you're feeling better, maybe you can convince my daughter to visit us more often," Betty said.

"Here comes the guilt trip," Shelly warned. "That only took five minutes. You beat your last record."

"Your father and I just miss you, that's all."

"How's everything?" Don was always the peacemaker between the two women in his life. "How's Brody? How's school?"

"Good and fine."

"Well, that was riveting information," he joked.

She shrugged. "There's not much to tell." She made eye contact with me, giving me a look that read: do not tell my parents that my boyfriend is planning to move in with me.

I gave her a look back that asked: what's the big deal?

"Here they go with the telepathic conversations, again." Don laughed and shook his head. "You girls have been doing that since you were five."

Betty wagged her finger. "That means there is news to discuss. What's so important that you can't tell your dear old parents?"

"I don't know what you're talking about." I shoved a forkful of spaghetti into my mouth.

Shelly did the same with her chicken.

"What about you, Merritt? Anything new with you?"

I shook my head and swallowed. "Same crap, different day."

"Have you decided when you're going to finish school?" Betty asked.

I twirled more spaghetti around my fork. "Not yet."

"She got a job, though," Shelly piped in.

Don raised his eyebrows. "Where?"

"At an auto body shop."

"Right up your alley! Which one?"

I shoved another forkful into my mouth, trying to stall my answer.

"At Tim's place," Shelly answered. "You remember Tim Brooks, right?"

"Oh, yeah. The one over on Rossville Avenue. That place gets a lot of business."

I nodded and chewed.

"Merritt and their eldest son, Chase, are friends. So he hooked her up with a job. She's been spending all her free time there – they're really busy."

I held my breath as Shelly explained everything to her parents. She was careful with her words. I suspected it was because she did not want me to out her secret about Brody moving in with her. She could keep her mouth shut when she needed to.

Betty looked skeptical. "Were you always friends with Chase? I don't remember you two being friendly when you were younger."

"Brody hangs out with him a lot. That's how we know each other," I lied.

Shelly nodded and tried to back me up. "We've all been trying to get Merritt out of the house lately. Cheer her up."

"A cute boy will do the trick." Betty winked at me.

"Oh, no. It's nothing like that," I quickly replied.

Don leaned back in his chair and patted his stomach. "Enough of this cute boy talk. Who wants salad?"

I took the salad bowl from him, and continued to shove forkfuls of food into my mouth.

"Merritt," Betty began. "You still have a box in the closet. Maybe you want to take a look through it, and see if there's anything you want to keep."

"Don't make her look through it now," Don interjected.

"It's okay," I waved my hand. I knew exactly which box she was talking about. "I'll just put it in Shelly's trunk and go through it another time." I stood quickly and began collecting the empty dishes, eager to escape this conversation before it continued.

Once the table was cleared off, I followed Shelly to the closet in Betty and Don's bedroom. She reached in and sat it gently on the floor in the middle of the room. It was labeled with my name on it in black marker.

"You shouldn't even look through it." Shelly flopped herself onto the bed. "You've been making a lot of progress lately. It might just stir up bad feelings and memories."

I sat on the floor, staring at the box. "I wish I could just throw it away. I can't bring myself to do it, though."

"I don't think you should throw it away. You might want those things later on in life. Just put it in the closet in your apartment. Or I can keep it at my place, if you want."

"No, it's okay." I picked at the tape that was curling on the side of the box. "Why didn't you want to tell your parents about Brody moving in?"

"They'll get all excited that we're taking the next step. I don't want them planning our wedding before we even get engaged."

"Have you guys talked about getting engaged?"

"Not really. We said we definitely need to finish school first. Get jobs. Maybe even a house."

I smiled. "I'm so proud of you, Shell."

She crinkled her nose. "Why do you say that?"

"Because look at your life – look how great it is."

"Your life will be great, too. I promise."

"Whatever my life is or isn't, I can still be happy for you. You deserve all the happiness in the world. You are my very best friend and I am so excited for you to take the next step in your relationship with Brody."

She smiled. "Thanks, Toad."

"Girls! Pie's out when you're ready!" Don called.

"Mmm. I love the smell of his apple pie."

"You should make more of an effort to come see them."

She rolled her eyes. "I know. I will."

"Seriously, Shell. Don't take them for granted."

She nodded, understanding where I was coming from.

I lifted the box off the floor. It was fairly light. The contents inside shuffled around as I stepped out into the hallway.

Chapter Twelve: Not So Saved by the Bell

"What's with the box?"

"It's a symbol of my procrastination and avoidance."

Chase's eyebrows lifted. "I can see that. It's been on the floor for weeks."

We sat on my couch after another tiresome day at work. His father had completely stopped going to the garage, and spent most of his days at home. I knew Chase was growing more worried by the day, so I tried to occupy him when we weren't working. Admittedly, he helped occupy my mind, too. With the holidays rapidly approaching, it was going to be a difficult time for the both of us.

"When I realized that my mom was never coming back, I decided to take any and all evidence of her out of sight. My dad couldn't handle seeing pictures of her, or anything else that reminded him of her."

"So you put it all in a box."

"Yup. So this is where it sits until I decide what to do with it."

"What are your thoughts?"

"Choice A, I can throw the whole thing out and forget all about it. Choice B, I open it and go through it, dealing with whatever emotions come about. I feel like Pandora."

He chuckled. "Pandora unleashed a lot of evil by opening that box. But that box also contained hope inside of it. Maybe if you go through everything in there, you will find some hope, and peace."

He always found a way of looking at things from a different perspective. It was something I admired about him. It made me want to look at everything through his lens, and see the world in a way I had never seen it before.

"Why are you looking at me like that?"

I sat up straight, unaware of the look on my face. "No reason."

"So, what do you think you want to do? I can bring it right outside to the trash, or you can open it up and deal with it. Either way, it's not good for you to sit here staring at it. You need to make a choice."

I took a deep breath. "I guess I'll go through it."

He stood and brought the box over to me, placing it on the floor in front of the couch. "I'll leave you to it, then."

I reached out and grabbed his arm. "Don't."

His eyebrows raised. "You want me to go through it with you?"

"Would you mind? I mean, you don't have to if you don't want–"

He sat down on the floor next to the box. "I'm ready when you are."

I scooted off the couch and sat on the floor, with the box in between us. My hand trembled slightly as I reached out to peel the tape back. Before the top flaps had even opened, I smelled a familiar scent wafting out. I picked up the blue glass perfume bottle that was lying on top of the pile, and set it on the floor. "This will be the garbage pile."

He nodded. "Garbage. Got it."

I lifted an old photo album out next. "Their wedding album. Also garbage."

"It's so weird to see the things she left behind. Like what made her decide to take certain things, but leave others? How did she choose?"

I shrugged. "Why she did the things she did will always be a mystery to me. I'll never know. Sometimes I think it's better this way. Not knowing."

Another album was next. I flipped through the pages to see if there were any photos worth saving.

"You look a lot like her," Chase said gently.

I nodded. "I used to wonder if that made it worse for my dad. To see her in me, like a constant walking reminder."

"I wonder if my mom will feel the same when she looks at me, after my dad is gone."

I looked up into his eyes that were filled with hurt. "Your mom will be reminded of what an amazing man he was whenever she looks at you."

He looked down at his lap.

I touched his arm. "I wish I could take away your pain."

"I feel the same way with you." He covered my hand with his, but could not bring his eyes to meet mine.

"You've helped me through the darkest time in my life. I can't ever thank you enough."

"You don't have to thank me." He averted his attention back to the box, reaching inside. He pulled out a folded piece of paper. "A note?"

I half laughed. "This was the note she left on the kitchen table when she disappeared."

He opened it and his mouth dropped open. "I'm sorry... that's it? Is she for real?"

"She's for real, alright." I took the note and slapped it on top of the garbage pile. "I guess she couldn't find the words to explain what a selfish piece of shit she was."

He shook his head. "That explains why you hate apologies so much."

I had never put the two together before.

Some CDs came out of the box next, and a pair of worn slippers after that. With them, I tossed aside birthday cards she had given me, and more pictures. At the very bottom sat a small black velvet box. I took it out and peeked at the ring inside.

"You should keep that," Chase suggested.

"I guess I could see how much it's worth."

"Not to pawn it. Your dad picked this ring out. He bought it with his own money, and with the love that he had for her. They created you with that love. This ring represents a lot."

"How did you get to be so insightful, Chase Brooks?"

He grinned. "What can I say? I was born a genius."

I rolled my eyes and smiled. "Okay, genius. That's the end of the box."

"Let me get all of this crap outside to the garbage." He stood and picked up the box. "Then we can order in if you want?"

"Ooh – let's order from that new sushi place that opened down the road."

"I'll eat whatever," he called as he was already halfway to the door.

Throwing away the contents of my former life was like a mental garbage day. Little by little, I was learning to make better choices for myself. My mother had abandoned me long ago, yet I was choosing to hold on to the pain; I was choosing to hold on to her leftovers. She was gone, and she was never coming back. Tonight, I chose to let go of the things that no longer served a purpose. I chose to give myself the closure I had never properly gotten. I chose happiness over the bitterness that I carried around with me for far too long.

"Goodbye," I said aloud to the empty room.

I pulled up the menu on my phone, and took a small pad out of one of the kitchen drawers. I walked over to Chase when he returned. "I have the menu up. Look over the menu and see what you want."

He took my phone and the pad from me and tossed them onto the couch.

"Hey, what are you –"

Before I could finish, he took my face into his hands and pressed his lips against mine. I was stunned, and could not do much else other than stand there and be kissed. His lips were warm and full. When he pulled back, his eyes searched mine, as if he was waiting for an answer to a question that I did not hear him ask. I could not move, I could not speak a word. We remained where we were. My heart was racing, unable to find my breath, and all I could hear was the sound of my pulse pounding in my ears.

Without wasting another second, I rose up onto my toes and met his lips with mine. His arms wrapped around me as he pushed me up against the wall. His moves were not aggressive, but deliberate; he did what he wanted in a way that was not forceful, but passionate. He cradled the back of my neck and pushed his tongue into my mouth. Though I could feel every part of him pressing against me, it did not feel close enough. I grabbed fistfuls of his hair to pull him closer. Kissing Chase Brooks felt exactly how one would expect it to feel. I could have kissed him for hours. I would have, if it weren't for the faint buzzing sound.

"What's that sound?" I breathed into his mouth.

He lifted me up and took me to the couch. His movements were smooth and effortless. "It's nothing," he murmured as he laid me down beneath him.

His tongue parted my lips and surged inside. I wrapped my legs around him, pressing his body against mine. I slid my hands under his shirt and ran my fingers along his smooth muscular back.

Then I heard it again.

"Something is buzzing. Is your phone in your pocket?"

He dropped his head onto my chest, and sighed out of frustration. "Yes."

I reached my hand into his pocket and pulled out his phone. "Chase, your mom called you three times. Tanner is calling you now!"

He instantly jumped to his feet and answered the call. "Hello? What's going on? What do you mean? You're heading there now? I'll meet you." He lowered the phone from his ear. "They're taking my dad to the hospital."

I sprang up from the couch. "Let's go."

He hesitated a moment, staring blankly at his phone.

"Come on. I'll drive if you want."

He shook his head. "No. I'll go alone."

I stopped in my tracks. "Oh. Okay. Are you sure? I can just drop you off if you want. I don't have to go in or anything."

"No, it's okay. I'll call you."

I wanted to reach out for his hand, but I held back. "I'll be here."

He turned around and walked out the front door. I stood there, waiting, unsure of what was going on – scared for what might be happening. Stranded without a car, I paced like a caged animal for the next twenty minutes, staring at my phone and willing it to ring with news about something. Anything. Anything but the worst.

Ring.

"Hello?"

"Whoa. It rang for literally half a second. What are you doing?"

"Shelly, where are you?"

"I'm at my place. Brody's working late tonight. Are you okay?"

"No. I mean yes, but no."

I could hear shuffling on the other end of the phone. "I'll be there in five."

In five minutes, Shelly walked through my open door. "You're pacing. That's never good. What the hell is going on?"

"Chase's dad… he's sick… they called, and he left to go to the hospital. But we kissed… and then he just left… and I… I don't know what to do now."

Shelly grabbed my shoulders and stopped me from pacing to look me in the eye. "You kissed Chase?"

I nodded. "We were supposed to get sushi. But I got kissed instead."

She fought back a smile as she released me. "What happened?"

"We were in the middle of kissing, and I heard his phone. It kept vibrating. I just knew something was wrong. Tanner called to let him know they were on the way to the hospital. I offered to go with him, but he said no. He said he would call. Why didn't he want me with him? He always wants me with him. Was it because we kissed? Was it because things are awkward now? Was the kiss not good to him? Should I call him? Should I go there?"

"Merr, stop. Stop pacing. Look at me."

I stopped and looked up at her. Tears began welling up in my eyes. "I don't know what to do. What if I made a mistake? What if the kiss ruined everything? I need to be there for him right now and he doesn't even want me there."

Shelly wiped the tears that began falling down my cheeks. "You didn't make a mistake. He kissed you because he has been wanting to kiss you for the past three months. Life just got in the way at the worst moment. Timing always sucks with these things. Why don't I drive you over there? We can sit together and wait."

"Can we? You wouldn't mind?"

"Of course not. Brody can meet us there after he gets off work. Chase needs friends right now. Do you know what's wrong with his dad?"

I nodded and looked down at the floor. "He has cancer. He's dying. That's why Chase had to come back from California."

Shelly covered her mouth with her hand. "Oh, no. Merritt..."

"Yeah. Let me go freshen up and we'll leave."

I blew my nose and wiped my eyes. I pulled a hoodie on over my head and stared at my reflection in the mirror. Hospitals brought back a lot of bad memories. I had to push past them, and do this for Chase. I took a deep breath and walked back into the living room.

"Let's go."

Chapter Thirteen: The Job

"Stay with me. Keep your eyes open. I need you to keep your eyes open!"

The voice sounded far away. I could feel that I was moving forward, but I did not know how. It felt like I was floating.

"No, Merritt. Don't close your eyes! I need you to keep them open. Look at me. Look in my eyes. Stay with me here."

I tried to listen to the voice and keep my eyes open, but the pain in my head was too severe. It felt better when I closed my eyes. Everything felt better when I closed my eyes and drifted off. The voice drifted off then, too. I began to float away.

I was suddenly startled by bright lights and loud noises. I was no longer floating, but speeding towards two big double doors. There were people all around me, pulling and prodding at me. I tried to speak, but began choking. Blood was spurting out of my mouth instead of words. I was terrified and confused. People were shouting over the sound of a rapid beeping in the background. A sharp pain went through my arm, and I tried to cry out for help.

"Merritt!"

I jolted upright at the sound of my name.

"Merr, wake up. You're having a nightmare."

"Brody?"

"Yes, it's Brody. Are you okay?"

I looked around at the empty waiting room. Brody sat next to me, with the same worried expression on his face that Shelly wore every time she woke me up from a nightmare.

"Where's Shelly?"

He pointed to the front desk. "She's trying to find out more information."

I pulled my phone out of my sweatshirt pocket. No missed calls. No texts.

"Anything?" he asked.

I shook my head.

"This is ridiculous," Shelly exclaimed. "We've been here for over an hour, and nobody can tell us anything. It's like déjà vu. Give me his number – I'm going to call him."

Brody took her hand and pulled her into the chair next to him. "Chase said he would call her. Give him some time. We don't know what is going on, if anything. He'll reach out when he's ready to."

"But he doesn't even know that we're here! He could have left, for all we know."

"He would have come through this door. His car is still parked outside. Just give it some more time." He kissed her forehead.

I was grateful that Brody came. Shelly was wound too tightly for me to handle right now. He would be able to reason with her, if anyone could.

"Are you okay?" she asked.

I nodded.

"Your nightmare again?"

"No. A different one actually."

She raised her eyebrows. "A different nightmare? About what?"

"I don't even know if it was a nightmare. I think… I think it was a memory."

"From the night of your accident?"

"I heard someone telling me to keep my eyes open. But I couldn't. I kept drifting off. Then it got loud, and there were a lot of people. I was in pain. I could hear beeping in the background."

"It sounds like the Emergency Room," Brody offered.

"Merr, who was telling you to keep your eyes open? Who did it sound like?"

"I couldn't make out the voice. It sounded garbled, and far away. Whenever I would try to speak, I would choke. I couldn't get the words out."

Brody shook his head. "Maybe it wasn't such a good idea, you coming here. I know this place brings back a lot of bad feelings for you."

"But she needs her memories to come back from her accident. Maybe this is exactly the place you need to be," Shelly countered.

I rested my head in my hand as I leaned on the armrest of the uncomfortable chair. "I just wish I knew if he was okay right now."

"I'm sure he's hanging in there. He's with his family." Brody reached out and touched my arm. "We could be here all night. I can stay with you, if you want to stay, or I can take you back home. It's your call."

"You guys don't have to stay. I'm not leaving until I see him."

Brody smiled. "I knew you were going to say that. I'll go see if they have any pillows or blankets."

Shelly scooted next to me while I checked my phone for the hundredth time. "He will call."

"I hate this place."

"I know. You've seen more of this place than anybody should in a lifetime."

Brody returned with two pillows and a blanket. He held them out in front of us.

"I'll just take a pillow. You guys can share the blanket." I tucked the pillow in between my head and the armrest. I stared at my phone, watching the minutes tick by. 11:06… 11:07… 11:08… My eyelids felt heavy. I let them close for just a moment.

"Merritt, wake up."

I picked my head up when I heard a gentle voice in my ear.

"Mrs. Brooks?" I blinked a few times to clear my eyes.

"It's Beverly, honey. What are you doing here? It's after midnight."

I sat up. "How is Tim? Is Chase okay?"

"Tim is stable for now. His body is weak, but he's fighting hard. Chase is upstairs. I can take you to him."

"He said he would call. I shouldn't go up yet."

"Don't be silly. He would love to see you. So would Khloe, and Tim when he wakes up. We'd all love to have you with us."

I looked over to Shelly and Brody. "Thanks for waiting here with me."

"We will take her home," Beverly said. "Thank you so much for coming."

Shelly stood and hugged her. "Let us know if you need anything."

"You're too kind."

I followed Beverly through the daunting familiar doors, and felt a tightening in my chest. I kept my eyes straight ahead, so as not to see anything or anyone around me.

She turned into room 303. I hesitated in the doorway. My palms were sweating, and I could feel my heart beating in my throat. Seeing Chase upset, seeing Tim lying there in bed, I was not prepared for any of it. I breathed in deep through my nose to calm my nerves, and shoved my hands into the pocket of my sweatshirt. They couldn't see me shaking. I had to hold it together for them. I needed to be strong for them.

I heard whispering, and then Chase appeared from behind the curtain that surrounded the bed. With sleep-deprived eyes and flattened hair, he looked exhausted. Still, he mustered a smile as he approached me at the doorframe.

"Are you expecting an earthquake, or are you going to come through the doorway?"

I would have laughed if it wasn't for the nervous knot in my stomach. "I… I don't know what to do."

"Come in. Khloe will be excited to see you."

I took another deep breath. I saw Khloe when I stepped into the room. She was sitting on Tanner's lap, who was in a chair next to the window. Her eyes lit up as she hopped off of Tanner, and ran to me with open arms. I scooped her up and squeezed her tightly.

"I can't breathe," she whispered.

I pressed my forehead against hers. "How are you doing, my pretty girl?"

"I'm okay. Daddy is not feeling well. He's tired, so he's taking a nap right now. You can see him when he wakes up."

Chase placed a chair behind me. I sat with Khloe in my lap. She leaned her head on my shoulder as she yawned a tiny human yawn. I looked around the room at everyone's faces. They were all wearing the same tired expression.

"Do you guys need me to get you anything? They have pillows and blankets. I can get you a cup of coffee, or tea?"

"Why don't you and I take a walk? We can get snacks for everyone," Chase offered.

"I would love a cup of hot tea, actually." Beverly held out her arms. "You can give her to me."

I stood with Khloe in my arms, and placed her in Beverly's lap. I looked to Tanner, who was mindlessly scrolling through his phone. "Do you want anything in particular?"

He shook his head without saying a word.

Back in the hallway, I kept my focus ahead, like a horse wearing blinders. We walked side-by-side in silence, turning corners and continuing down the next hallway. The pounding inside my head was so loud that I worried Chase could actually hear it.

"How long have you been here for?" he asked quietly.

"Since nine-thirty, I think. I know you didn't want me here. I was just worried. If you want me to leave, I can have Shelly take me home. I just—"

He stopped walking and turned to face me. "Why would you think I don't want you here?"

"You said you didn't want me to come with you when Tanner called."

"I only said that because I didn't think you wanted to come to the hospital. I know you've seen enough of this place with your accident. I thought it would be hard for you."

I breathed a sigh of relief as I stared up into his beautiful tired eyes. "How is your dad?"

"The doctor said that his body is slowing down. He's been fighting this for so long. I don't know how much he's got left in him."

I looked down at my feet as we started walking again. There were no words to say that could make this better. To make matters worse, things between us felt awkward – forced. I was unsure of how he felt after our kiss. It wasn't the right time to bring it up, I knew, but my nerves would not simmer down until we talked about it. I wasn't even sure what it all meant. Were we physically attracted to each other, or was it more than that? Would he want to be together, or keep it platonic? I tried to stay in the moment, and be present for Chase and his family.

In the café, he picked out a few items for Khloe and Tanner while I filled cups with coffee and tea. We were silent again on our walk back to the room. When we arrived, he stopped just outside the door. "I don't want to stay in this room anymore. Let's drop this stuff off and go sit in that area by the big window."

"Sure." I walked inside the room and handed Beverly her tea. Khloe was asleep in her arms. I set a cup of coffee on the windowsill next to Tanner. I didn't bother to say anything, knowing he wouldn't respond anyway.

"We're going to be down the hall," Chase whispered to his mother. "Call me if you need me."

She nodded her head and reached out for my hand. "Thank you for being here," she whispered.

I held on to her hand tightly before letting go and following Chase out the door.

We sat beside each other, staring out the big windows in the waiting area. The sky was pitch black in the dead of night, the moon covered by clouds. Chase watched the traffic below coming and going, while I watched his reflection in the window pane.

"What floor were you on when you were here?" His question finally broke the silence.

"Which time?"

"What do you mean? When else were you here?"

"My dad… he had lost so much blood when I came home and found him. I called 911 immediately and they rushed him to the hospital here. I didn't expect them to, honestly. By the time they arrived, I had already accepted the fact that he was gone. In the ambulance they tried to keep him alive, but I knew he wouldn't make it. Part of me didn't want him to make it. It was obviously what he wanted, to die. I told him I loved him, and that I understood. I told him it was okay to leave me. By the time we got to the Emergency Room, he was gone."

Chase's eyes were filled with tears. I knew he was imagining how he would handle it when his father's time came. "How did you do it? You were all alone. How did you handle that by yourself?"

"Obviously I didn't handle it too well. I ended up in the hospital myself just a few days later."

"You did the best you could. You're still doing it now. You wake up every single day, tired from the demons you faced the night before, and you keep fighting. You lost your family. I don't know how you survived."

"I don't know either. Getting through tough times is something that nobody ever teaches you how to do. You either pick yourself up, or you don't." I covered his hand with mine. "You will. You have your family – you will get through it together. It doesn't seem like it now, but you will."

"You'd think I would be ready for this. He's been sick for so long, we've been preparing for this moment. I just keep feeling like I need more time."

"Just because you know the outcome, doesn't make you ready for it. Nothing can prepare you to lose your father."

He quickly swiped a tear away with his thumb. "I didn't know you found your dad… like that."

I nodded and stared out the window at the sliver of the moon that was peeking out from behind the dark clouds. "I had called him on my way home from school that day. I was going to ask if he wanted anything particular for dinner that night. He didn't eat much towards the end, so I figured if I could make him something he loved, it would perk him up a little. Sounds so stupid now."

"It's not stupid. You were trying."

"He didn't pick up, which was normal. I didn't see him on the couch when I walked in, so I checked his bedroom. He slept a lot. I walked right past the bathroom. When he wasn't in his bed, I realized the bathroom door was half-opened. He hadn't showered in days, so I was actually excited that he might be in there cleaning up. He was lying in the tub." I shook my head. "There was just so much blood."

"Merritt, I am so unbelievably sorry that you had to see that."

"I didn't cry. I think I was too stunned by it. I knew he couldn't go on like that forever. I often wondered how it would end."

"You didn't cry at the funeral, either."

I turned my head to look at him. "How did you know that?"

"I was there. My parents were, too."

"Oh, God. I didn't know that. You guys didn't need to be there."

"My parents were going. I had just gotten back from California when I heard the news. I felt terrible for you. I knew you my whole life. To watch someone going through something like that… it feels awful."

"So I guess you saw everything that happened that night." I looked down at my lap. It was embarrassing to think about how drunk everyone had seen me, let alone knowing that Chase had witnessed it, too.

He nodded. "I did. I wanted to stop you from leaving. I often think about what would have happened if I could have stopped you. Maybe you wouldn't have been in that accident."

"I don't think anyone could have stopped me. I was so angry, and drunk. It was my own fault."

"I don't know why we have to go through these things."

"Nobody knows. But you have me – I will help you through it. I didn't think I was up for the job when you first told me about your dad being sick. But over time, I understood why you wanted to be friends."

"What do you mean?" His eyebrows were furrowed. "What job?"

"I couldn't figure out why you were suddenly talking to me, and offering to drive me to therapy." I laughed. "I mean, come on. We never spoke all those years in school."

His eyes tightened. "You think I've been talking to you all this time just because my dad is dying? You think of this – of me – as a job?"

"No. That part came out wrong. I just figured you wanted help from someone who went through something similar. Why else would you be talking to me?"

"Gee, Merritt. I don't know. It can't possibly be because I have feelings for you. Because you can't accept something like that in your life, right? No, it must be because I'm using you as my therapist. That makes total sense." He stood. "Why do you think I kissed you tonight? Did you take that as that some form of payment for your services?"

I jumped to my feet. "Chase, no. You're getting it all mixed up."

"No. You're the one who has it all mixed up. I have been trying so hard to prove myself to you – to show you that I'm not playing games, and to show you that you can trust me. I actually thought I was getting somewhere. I thought… I thought you felt the way I do. But no. You were just trying to help me. You felt bad for me."

"No, stop. You're not listening to me."

"You know, you've been making yourself clear all this time, and I just didn't listen. I thought you were going through a rough time, and I just had to be patient for you to see what we have. But I guess it's time I start hearing what you've been telling me all along."

"Everything is coming out wrong. Please just sit and let me fix this."

"I can't do this right now. My father is dying in the room back there – I need to focus on what is important."

"Okay. You're right. We can save this for another time." I took my phone out of my pocket. "I'll call a cab or something."

Chase rubbed his eyes and ran his fingers through his hair. "You don't have to leave. My mom was so excited that you came." He looked down at his feet. "My dad didn't even get to see you, yet."

"You tell me what you want me to do, and I'll do it. If you want me to leave, I'll go. If you want me to stay, I'm here."

"Stay." He sighed and turned to walk back to the room without another word.

I followed. All I wanted to do was run into the bathroom and cry. I was stunned at the turn the conversation had taken, and how angry he was. I had not seen Chase like that before, and I did not know how to react. I needed to figure out a way to smooth things over, but not now. I had to wait for a better time. As I walked into room 303, I wasn't sure when that better time would come.

Chapter Fourteen: Peace Pie

"Hello? Earth to Merritt."

I looked up at the sound of my name. "Huh?"

"Can you please pass the gravy?"

"Oh. Sorry." I lifted the plastic bowl in front of me and handed it to Don.

"Where did you go?" he asked gently.

"Nowhere. Just thinking."

"Uh-oh," Betty chimed in. "What's his name?"

Shelly entered the room with a bottle of wine. "His name is Chase Brooks, and he has left her like this for two weeks now."

"What did he do?"

"He didn't do anything. He's just going through a hard time right now." I shot Shelly a look for bringing this up to her parents.

"Again I ask – what did he do?" Betty was always quick to defend us against any prospective boys.

"Really. Nothing."

Shelly rolled her eyes. "He has been pursuing Merritt since the summer. She's been in denial about it the entire time. Two weeks ago, he finally grows some balls and kisses her – the same night his dad ends up in the hospital. She rushes over to be with him, and they get into a dumb fight. Now, it's Thanksgiving and they still haven't made up. I don't care if he's going through something right now – he's being a stubborn idiot."

"Shelly," I warned. "He's not an idiot."

"Oh, she's defending him," Don noted to Betty. "That means it's serious."

"No, no." I waved my hands. "Can we just change the subject please? I don't want to talk about it at dinner."

"She doesn't want to talk about it. It is serious." Betty winked at Don.

"Thanks, Shell," I muttered. It was bad enough that Chase and I were barely speaking. It was embarrassing to have it broadcasted during holiday dinner.

"What was the fight about?" Don asked.

I sighed. "I offended him with something I said."

He shrugged. "You offend everybody with the things you say. It's all part of the Adams appeal."

I cracked a smile. "I wasn't meaning to be sarcastic that time. I genuinely hurt his feelings. I just don't know how to make it better. Plus, his dad has been in and out of the hospital lately."

"Where she has been by his side night and day," Shelly added.

"It sounds like he just needs some time. Keep being there for him. You're doing the right thing." Don reassured me with a gentle hand squeeze.

"Where are they today?" Betty asked. "Not at the hospital, I hope."

"No. They're home. His dad's health is going to be up and down for a while, according to the doctors."

"And where's the Brodster? I thought he was coming to dinner with you." Don always liked having another male around to balance out the estrogen.

Shelly sighed dramatically. "His sister is in town with her tribe of kids, so he said he would stop by after for pie."

"Mm pie." I could drool at the thought of Betty's homemade pumpkin pie.

"Maybe you could take some pie over to your boyfriend's house later."

I shot Betty a look. There was no question where Shelly got her persistence from.

"What? It would cheer him up. I think it's a nice gesture."

"Pie is a sign of peace," Don stated with a smile.

After being with Chase so much these past few months, it was weird barely speaking the way we were now. If we were working, we were in our designated corners trying to keep up with the flow of customers. If we were at the hospital, we were with his family. When I wasn't thinking about the fight, I was thinking about the kiss. It was an unmerry-go-round of torture, and all I wanted to do was get off.

At the end of the night, I took my leftovers out of the car and waved to Shelly.

"Looks like you have a visitor," she pointed.

I turned around to see Chase sitting on my top step. He stood as I started up the stairs, holding a plate wrapped in foil. My heart was racing as acid sloshed into my stomach. I was excited, yet nervous.

"You brought peace pie, too."

"What's peace pie?" he asked, a slight hint of a smile on his face.

I handed him the small container filled with Betty's pumpkin pie. "Apparently pie is a sign that you come in peace. If only the Pilgrims had known that." I unlocked the door and pushed it open.

He followed me inside and perched himself on the armrest of the couch, his leg shaking restlessly. He held up the foil covered plate. "Truce?"

"That depends on how good this pie is."

He grinned.

My heart didn't merely skip a beat – it pole-vaulted out of my chest. I didn't realize just how much I missed seeing his smile. It was a sign that all would be okay. I took the plate from him, and grabbed a fork from the kitchen drawer. I sat on the recliner and uncovered the plate. On it was a slice of blueberry pie.

"Did your mom make this?"

He nodded. "Khloe helped. She wanted me to bring you a slice."

"At least one of the Brooks siblings still cares about me." I shoved a huge bite of pie into my mouth.

"This sibling still cares about you, too."

I took my time chewing, in the hopes that he would keep talking. I was unsure of how to navigate this conversation. After what transpired the last time we spoke, I was afraid of saying anything at all.

"I know you don't like apologies, so I'm not sure how else to say this… but I am sorry for blowing up on you. I just…" He ran his fingers through his hair. "I didn't like what you said."

I nodded.

"I know you said that it came out wrong, and you didn't mean it."

"I didn't," I said, with pie still smooshed in my mouth.

"It didn't feel good to hear that you only let me into your life because you heard my father was sick and you felt bad. It hurt to hear that you looked at me as a job. Isn't that exactly how you felt, thinking everyone felt bad for you and did things for you out of pity?"

I placed the dish down on the coffee table in front of me. "You're right. I never thought of it that way."

"You don't think of things in any way except your own. You hold onto your convictions so tightly, that you can't see any other possibilities out there except for the one you've conjured up in your head. It's really frustrating."

"I'm sorry that I'm so frustrating to you."

"You are unbelievably frustrating!" He stood and walked towards me. "You're obstinate and passive-aggressive. You're rude."

"I am not rude!" I stood to meet him in the middle of the living room.

"You are to me!"

"Well, I am so sorry that you have had to put up with me for all this time. Did you come here just to tell me what a horrible person I am?"

"I did, actually. I came here to tell you what an asshole you have been to me. You push me away, then you pull me back in. You think your sarcasm covers up your feelings, but it doesn't. You wear your heart on your sleeve and your emotions on your face. I know who you are, and despite all of that, I am standing here madly in love with you. I just wish you could admit that you love me back."

My jaw could have been scraped off the floor with a shovel, like in one of those old cartoons. "You can't stand me, but you love me? How am I even supposed to take all of that?"

"I'm in love with you, Merritt." He took my face into his hands. "I'm crazy about you. All I want is for you to say you feel the same way."

Staring up into his golden splattered eyes, as I had done so many times before, I knew I had to tell the truth. I knew it was not the time for sarcasm and jokes. It was not the time for evading. I had run to the end of the line. I had no choice but to face it all – my fears, my demons, and him. I put my hands on his wrists, and gently pulled them away from my face.

"I know I'm frustrating. I know I'm hard to love. I've always felt like I was never good enough for anyone. I know you feel like I don't let you in. I know you feel like I have pushed you away. But for me, it hasn't been that way at all. I have let you into my life, and into my heart. You have opened my eyes to different perspectives, and made me second-guess my beliefs and opinions. You have helped me get through the worst time. You helped me remember how to smile again. If it weren't for you, I'd still be sitting on Shelly's recliner having nightmares. You have changed everything for me, and for that I will be eternally grateful. Being around you is not a job. It is a desire. You are a beautiful human, inside and out. You are perfection… and I know I can never measure up to the person you are." A tear rolled down my cheek.

He held my stare dubiously. "What are you saying?"

"I'm saying… I can never measure up to the person you are, but I can love you with my whole heart… and I hope that can count for something."

"You love me?"

I swiped the tear from my face. "I do."

His lips crashed into mine, and all hope for further conversation was lost.

I walked him backwards to the couch, and pulled him down on top of me. We picked up where we had last left off, with my legs wrapped around his body. My mouth begged for his tongue as he teased me with it, slowly and intently tracing my lips. I slid his shirt up to feel the ripple of his abs on my fingertips. He lifted me up and sat me on top of him, changing positions in one swift motion. I felt him through his jeans while he took two handfuls of my ass and pressed me against him. Every part of my body yearned to be touched by him, and where it had been touched tingled with excitement. Our tongues swirled around one another, and I lost track of time as we traveled to a place that seemed so far away from where we were.

We both crashed down to Earth when we heard the knock at my door.

I whined as he slid me off of his lap. "Is this going to happen every time?!"

"It better not," he grumbled as he flung open the door. I saw his face soften immediately.

"Did Merry like the pie?" My favorite tiny human stepped through the entryway. She ran to me when she spotted me on the couch. "Did you try the pie yet?"

I smiled and hugged her. "I did. It was the best pie I have ever tasted. Thank you for saving me a slice."

Khloe pulled back from my embrace. "Why are you so sweaty?" She looked up at Chase, who was now standing beside the couch. "Your cheeks look red."

I stifled a laugh. "I hope we're not getting sick!"

"Does mom know where you are right now?" the concerned big brother asked.

She nodded her head feverishly. "I told her. Do you think we can have a sleepover tonight, Merry? I don't have school tomorrow."

My eyes widened. "You don't? We should definitely have that sleepover tonight then!"

Chase chuckled. "Why don't you guys have the sleepover in your room, Khlo?"

She jumped up and down excitedly. "I have a tumble bed! It pulls out from the bottom!"

I laughed. "A trundle bed? That's awesome. Why don't I pack some things, and meet you over there in about five minutes? You can get your pajamas on while you're waiting!"

Khloe ran towards the door. "See you in five minutes!"

"She could have slept here. I don't mind." I closed the door behind her.

Chase pulled me in for another kiss. "But if you're at my house, you can come into my room once she is asleep."

I smacked him playfully. "I can't let your parents see me sleeping in your room."

"Who said anything about sleeping?" He grinned as he stepped outside and swung the door closed.

My skin was still humming as I threw several sleepover essentials into a backpack. I hoped Chase was joking, as we had only just begun telling each other how we felt. What did it all mean? What did it make of us? We were in love, but love makes people do crazy things. Surely it would not happen tonight, in the presence of his sleeping family members. But every interruption only built up more anticipation. Were we ready for a physical relationship? Was I?

I pushed these questions from my mind as I knocked on the Brooks' door. Khloe greeted me, wearing zebra-striped footie pajamas.

"Slumber party! Slumber party! Slumber party!" she screamed, while jumping up and down.

Beverly poked her head out of the living room, smiling as always. "Come on in, Merritt. We're about to have a movie night."

"What are we watching?" I whispered to Khloe, who had taken my backpack and my hand as she led me into the living room.

"It's Moana!"

"Take it down a notch, slappy." Tanner covered his ears. I was pleasantly surprised to see him there. It was a sign he was making an attempt to spend time with his family.

"Let's pretend like we're in the movies," I whispered.

"Good idea," she whispered back. "You can sit here, next to me and Chase."

"Best seat in the house," Chase whispered.

"Kokomo, show Merritt how she can recline her seat," Tim called from his spot next to Beverly. He looked tired, as usual, but happy as always.

"Got it," she responded.

"Tanner, you didn't strike me as the Moana type," I smirked.

"Oh, you just wait until my song comes on."

Khloe giggled, clearly in on the joke. She laid with her head on my lap.

Chase interlocked his fingers with mine, and planted a kiss on my hand. As the movie began, I rested my head against his shoulder.

My heart felt full and content with the Brooks family. I tried hard to pretend like the imminent storm was out of sight. The family puzzle would be left with a missing piece as Tim's cancer progressed, and it was too difficult to think about. I focused on the movie, and the sleepy angel laying in my lap.

When the movie ended, Tim instructed Khloe to get ready for bed. "Merritt can tuck you in when you're ready."

"Let's brush our teeth together," she whispered as I followed her up the stairs.

I giggled. She wanted a true slumber party, and I would oblige.

After we swished and spit, Khloe showed me to her room. It was an explosion of pink and purple. I smiled as I looked at her baby pictures perched atop her dresser.

"This is my bed," she gestured. "And this is yours. We're like sisters!"

"I've always wanted a sister." I tucked her under the covers. "Thanks for letting me stay in your room. I love it in here."

"Thanks." She yawned while I ran my fingers through her hair. I watched her eyes slowly close, and then pop open again. "Goodnight, Merry. I'll see you in the morning. Chase is making breakfast he said."

"Goodnight, angel girl. See you for pancakes."

In five minutes, she was asleep. I jumped when I turned to realize that Tim was standing in the doorway. He grinned when he saw that he had scared me. I closed Khloe's door behind me, and stood with him in the hallway.

"She loves you. She looks up to you, you know."

"She's precious. You guys did a great job raising your kids. You have three really great ones."

Tim nodded, and folded his arms across his chest. "You're one of the great ones, too, Merritt. I hope you know how highly we all think of you."

"Thank you. That means a lot."

"You are a part of our family now. It feels good to know that Chase has you to lean on. I've never seen him this way before. I'm glad it's someone like you."

Beverly emerged from the bathroom. "Come to bed, dear. Goodnight, Merritt. Chase is right in there." She pointed to the room next door to Khloe's.

"Night. Thanks." I felt awkward stepping into Chase's room in front of his parents. I fought back a smile as I entered, surrounded by a sea of navy-colored walls. I looked around at the Yankee memorabilia hanging on his walls, with several football trophies displayed on a shelf. I wondered if this is exactly what his room looked like back in high school.

"What is so funny?" he asked, sitting on the edge of his bed.

"Your mother just directed me to your room." I covered my face in embarrassment. "It's funny that I'm even here, in Chase Brooks' bedroom. The old me would never believe it."

He pulled lightly on my arm, until I was standing inches from his face. "I can barely believe it now."

I stroked his soft hair, and kissed his forehead.

He placed his hand over my heart. "It's beating so fast."

"It always beats like this when I'm around you."

"Do I make you nervous?" He moved my hair away from my neck, and began making a trail of light kisses from my jawline to my collarbone. "Or excited?"

"A little of both," I exhaled.

"What are you nervous about?" He kissed his way across my chest, and I felt his tongue along the other side of my neck.

"What we're going to do."

He sat up straight and looked into my eyes as he spoke. "We don't have to do anything. I just want to kiss you, uninterrupted. I want to lie here and hold you tonight, and wake up with you in my arms. Is that okay?"

"It's perfect."

He pulled me into his embrace and kissed me. I craved his lips like I was lost in the desert searching for water. I was dying of thirst, and he was all I needed to survive. Once I had him, I couldn't get enough. We kissed into the late hours of the night, until our motions slowed and our eyelids felt heavy.

"Let's get under the covers," he whispered.

As I slid my legs under his sheets, he stood. I watched him slip his shirt up and over his head, revealing his flawlessly ripped torso. My eyes made their way over his smooth chest and perfectly formed abs; they continued on to the protruding bones that seemed to point the way down his pelvis. I could not avert my eyes when he pulled down his jeans, and waltzed over to the light switch in his tight-fitting boxer briefs. His body was a work of art. He could have beaten Mark Wahlberg out of his underwear ad circa 1991.

"Hey. Leave the light on for a little longer," I whispered.

He looked down as he grinned, running his fingers through his hair.

I sat up on my knees as he walked back to the bed. "Chase Brooks, are you nervous?" I planted several kisses on his chest, and ran my fingers over his stomach. "Or excited?"

"A little of both."

I smiled. "Good." I continued kissing every inch of bare skin on his body. Every now and then I would sit back on my heels to take his body into full account. "You may turn off the lights now."

He switched them off and climbed into bed beside me. My head fell into that perfect spot in the crook of his neck, as he wrapped his arms around me. With our bodies intertwined beneath the sheets, I inhaled slowly and deeply. My racing heart began to slow down.

"I could lay in this moment forever," he whispered softly into my ear.

If only we could.

Chapter Fifteen: Humiliation with a Side of Awkwardness

The next morning, we woke up in exactly the same position. I felt wetness on my mouth that I realized to be drool. Mortified, I quickly wiped it away, double-checking to see that Chase was still asleep. I slipped out of bed, and made a mad dash to the bathroom. I brushed my teeth, wiped the crust from my eyes, and tried to smooth down the Medusa-like snakes that were slithering out of my bun. Beverly and Tim's door was open, but all of the other doors were still shut. I tiptoed back to Chase's room, and slipped under the covers.

He reached for me, his eyes still closed, and pulled me into his warm embrace. "I had the best sleep ever," he murmured with his face buried in the pillow.

I smiled, running my fingers through his smooshed-allover hair. "I did, too, actually."

His eyes sprang open. "Did you have your nightmare?"

I shook my head. "Nope. I slept through the entire night."

A huge grin swept across his face. "It's settled then."

"What's settled?"

"You should sleep with me every night. I'm the cure for all of your bad dreams."

I smiled, and began planting kisses all over his face.

"Is that a smile that says yes, Chase, I will sleep with you every night?"

I flipped him over onto his back and began kissing his chest. "It's a smile that says don't get ahead of yourself, buddy."

"Says the girl who has fully mounted me in my bed."

"You should be shirtless more often." I thought about my suggestion, and amended it. "Around me, that is."

"I feel the same way about you." He slipped his hand under my t-shirt.

I slowly rocked my hips against him. "I have to admit, I wouldn't mind waking up to this every morning."

"I want you so bad."

"I can feel that," I whispered.

Before I could stop him, he had my shirt up and over my head, and flipped me onto my back. "Chase! Your door is unlocked!"

"Nobody's coming in here," he mumbled as he began licking his way down my body.

His tongue traveling along my stomach sent a warm sensation all the way down to my toes. He lingered near the elastic on my pajama pants, like a dog pacing near the door to be let outside.

I pulled him back up to my lips just in time as his door swung wide open. He flung the covers over us, hiding the fact that I was topless underneath.

"Time to get up, sleepyheads!" Khloe pranced into the room. I held my breath, praying to the gods that this kid would not try to snuggle in bed with us. "Are you going to make pancakes, Chasey?"

"Yeah, just give me a few minutes to wake up."

"Fine. But hurry! I'm hungry!" She pranced back out of the room, closing the door behind her.

I giggled, sliding my hand against his boxers. "Oh, I think you're awake."

He groaned in my ear. "You're killing me, Merr."

"Good. Now get my shirt, before another one of your family members burst in here like you said they wouldn't."

Downstairs, Khloe and I set the table while Chase cooked breakfast for everyone. Tim and Beverly were going through Christmas decorations, getting ready to put their tree up. Surprisingly, Tanner was helping them. It was a genuine morning with family.

"Merry, are you going to put your tree up today?"

"No. I don't have a tree."

"We need to get you one," Chase called from the kitchen.

"Don't need one," I called back.

"You need to get one!" Khloe cried. "How is Santa going to come if you don't have a tree?"

"She's got you there," Tanner yelled from the living room.

"Maybe you boys should quit yelling, and go get her a tree," Tim called back.

"Sure, take her side," Tanner laughed. It was strange seeing him wearing an expression other than his usual angry grimace.

"Breakfast is ready!" Khloe squealed. She followed Chase out of the kitchen and into the dining room.

"Wow, babe." I plopped in the chair next to Khloe. "This is impressive."

"Guess you have to be screwing Chase to get a meal outta him." Tanner smirked.

"Tanner!" both Tim and Chase shouted.

My eyes widened, and my cheeks burned. "No. We're not... I didn't..."

"What does screwing mean?" Khloe asked.

"I swear, I wish you were little so I could still put you into time out!" Beverly ran her fingers through her hair, the same way Chase does when he is stressed. "Don't listen to him, Merritt."

"Calm down. I'm just joking. Merritt gets it," Tanner mumbled.

"It doesn't matter if she gets it or not. It's inappropriate." Chase's jaw was clenched, and his hands were balled into fists under the table. Chase definitely had a temper, and Tanner seemed to be one of the only few people who could turn it on like the flick of a switch.

"What is your deal lately? You have a girlfriend, now. Shouldn't you be in a better mood instead of worrying about what I say and do all the time?"

"Boys," Beverly warned.

"I wouldn't have to worry about the things you say and do if you got your act together and stopped acting like a douchebag!" Chase fired back.

"Boys!" Tim slammed his fist on the table. "Enough of this crap! You're in the presence of women. You don't conduct yourselves like this!"

"You shouldn't act like this even if you're not in the presence of women!" Beverly added. "You two have been at each other's throats, and I've had enough of it."

Khloe and I chewed silently, waiting for the brothers' reprimanding to be over. I felt bad that Tanner was getting yelled at when he thought he was joking around with me. I could handle his banter, but bringing up sex in front of his parents, especially after just having spent the night in Chase's room, made me want to crawl under a rock and disappear.

Both of the Brooks brothers had their heads down after being scolded by their parents. It was painfully awkward.

"Well, that was fun," I began. "Humiliation with a side of awkwardness always goes great with pancakes and bacon in the morning, don't you think?"

Tim was the first one to break a smile. "You have nothing to be embarrassed about. We're not reading into what Tanner said."

Chase rubbed my knee under the table. "I'm sorry."

"Don't be."

He shook his head. "I don't think I'll ever get used to that response whenever I apologize."

I shrugged. "You're gonna have to."

Tanner's eyes lifted. "What response?"

"I hate apologies. They mean nothing. They're just words. Don't try to take back something you did. Own it. You did what you did, or said what you said, for a reason. Why bother being sorry about it?"

Tanner nodded, and I could see the wheels spinning in his mind.

"But what if someone's really sorry for what they did, Merry?"

I laughed. "You and your brother are so alike, it's scary."

Chase puffed out his chest proudly. "You're one lucky kid."

Tanner and I made eye contact and exchanged overdramatic eye rolls.

After breakfast was cleaned up, I packed my things to head back to my apartment.

"We're going to start decorating the tree. Why don't you stay?" Beverly offered.

"That's really kind of you, but I'm going to Shelly's to help her decorate her tree. It's a tradition we have… the only family tradition I have left, really."

Tanner strode into the room and laid out on the couch. "So start a new one, with us."

My eyebrows almost reached my hairline when they shot up in surprise. "You want me to stay?" I started poking his midsection. "Are you going to miss me, Tanner?"

Khloe immediately ran over to join in, and jumped full-force on top of him. He pretended to wrestle her, causing her to let out her high-pitched squeal.

I hugged Tim and Beverly, thanking them for letting me stay over. Chase walked me outside.

"I'm just going to say it one last time." He ran his fingers through his hair. "I'm sorry I got so angry with Tanner in front of you before."

"I don't care that you did it in front of me. I can handle an alpha male pissing contest. What you should be sorry for is getting like that in front of your parents. You guys shouldn't be upsetting your dad right now."

He nodded, looking down at his socks on the concrete.

I caressed his cheek softly. "I appreciate you coming to my defense. I know that's all you were trying to do." I frowned. "That was definitely mortifying. I don't want your parents to think we had sex in their house."

He grinned, pulling me closer to him. "Sleepover at your place tonight, then?"

I nodded, losing all focus with his lips brushing against mine.

"I love you," he breathed.

"And I love you."

Even though it was a cold November day, my entire body felt like it was burning up as I walked into my apartment. I turned on the shower, twisting the knob to all the way to cold.

Chapter Sixteen: When the Time is Right

"I can't," I said.

"Yes, you can," said the voice.

"I'm stuck." I coughed again, choking more with every breath. "My arm."

"I will get you out of here, but you need to help me. Pull yourself out. Ready? Pull!"

I leaned toward the voice. A splitting pain shot through my shoulder. I tried to scream in pain, but the smoke was so thick, I could not inhale.

"Don't stop! Keep pulling!"

"It hurts!" I choked, and kept pulling. The flames were so close, it felt like I was melting from the heat.

"Stop looking at the fire – now pull! Pull as hard as you can!"

I squeezed my eyes shut and pulled, mustering all of my might to make one last effort.

"Merritt! Get in here!"

I sat up in my bed.

Shelly peeked her head through the slightly opened bedroom door. "Did you hear me?"

"I think Mars heard you, Shell. Give me a sec." I rubbed the sleepiness from my eyes, and tried to catch my breath.

"Are you still having nightmares? Merr–"

I held my hand up. "Each one is filled with more and more detail."

"It's like your mind is trying to put the pieces together. Did you see anyone yet?"

I shook my head. "Now what is it that you were yelling about?"

She took my hand and dragged me down the hall. "This!"

In my living room, standing before me, was a Christmas tree. It was short, about my height, and decorated with colorful lights and red bows. There was a single ornament hanging from one of the branches. It was a 1970 cherry red Chevelle – an exact replica of my old car. On another nearby branch, a note was dangling with the words "Open Me" written across it.

"Chase did this while you were sleeping. How romantic!" Shelly cooed.

I smiled as I took the note off the tree. "He is a romantic."

"Has he been around more?"

"Nope. He's still staying after hours at the shop. I try to stay and help, but he just shoos me out. I'm starting to think it's me."

"No way." Shelly bounced onto the couch. "He's definitely overwhelmed with taking over his dad's business, especially with Christmas right around the corner."

I sat on the couch next to her, and unfolded the note: You know I wouldn't let you get away with not having a tree for Christmas… even though your gift won't quite fit under there. Meet me at the shop tonight at seven. I love you.

Shelly squealed in excitement as she read the note over my shoulder.

I held my ear in pain. "And there goes my eardrum."

"Sounds like he's going to make up for all the lost time." She nudged me playfully. "Maybe tonight will be the night."

"No, tonight is not the night."

"But he just gave you a Christmas tree!"

"So now I have to have sex under it?"

"You're going to have to give it up to him eventually, you know."

"Yes, I know. I will do it when I'm ready to. We've only been dating a few weeks, Shell. Relax. Maybe you're the one who needs to go get laid."

"I am in a healthy sexual relationship. My vagina is extremely happy, thank you very much."

"Good. I'm glad for you and your vagina." I stood and walked to my room to get dressed.

"My vagina feels sad for your vagina," she called down the hallway.

"My vagina just gave your vagina the finger," I yelled back.

I heard her giggling from the living room and I smiled. Chase was preoccupied lately, but I was not worried about the lack of attention. Though his dad was not doing well, he was still here. His family would get to spend Christmas together, and I understood how important that was. Though I had told him that I did not want a tree, he insisted, and I think it was more for him than anything else. If he focused on getting me through my first Christmas without my dad, it would somehow get him through his last Christmas with his.

I helped Shelly pick out presents for Brody and her family the rest of the day. It helped pass the time until meeting Chase at seven. It was odd that he asked me to meet him at work, but I did not care as long as I got to spend some time with him.

"There's my girl." A huge smile spread across Chase's face when I walked through the garage door promptly at seven o'clock.

I wrapped my arms around him. "Thank you for the tree."

"Do you like it?"

"I love it. It was very thoughtful of you."

"If you think that was thoughtful, wait until you see what I have for you next." He pulled me over to the far end of the garage. We approached a car under a beige tarp that had been sitting in the same spot for months. Chase looked nervous as he rubbed his hands together and looked at me.

"I know I haven't been around much lately," he began. "I have been working on this project for five months, and I've been putting the finishing touches on it the past couple of weeks. Now that it's done I want to show you."

"Oh, cool. How come you haven't let me help you with it?"

"What kind of boyfriend would I be if I made you work on your own Christmas present?"

My eyebrows pushed together in confusion. "What do you mean?"

He tugged at the bottom of the tarp, and slowly uncovered the vehicle hidden beneath it.

My hands flew up to my mouth in complete and utter shock. I could not take my eyes off of it. I stepped closer to get a better look, as if it was not real – as if the ghost of my father himself was standing before me.

Chase stood quietly, holding the tarp the way a nervous child holds his blanket.

"Where did this come from? How did you get this?"

He let the tarp fall to the floor, and took my hands into his. "After your accident, the car was being taken to the junk yard. I did not have the heart to let them throw away your car. So, I had it towed here. My dad helped me find all the parts we needed to rebuild it. I worked on it a little each day. Even Tanner worked on it at times. I wanted to have it ready sooner, but everything with my dad started happening. I had to work on it a little extra these past few weeks so that it would be ready in time for Christmas."

I could feel the tears spilling down my face, but I could not stop them – nor did I care. I kept staring at my Chevelle in disbelief.

"Are those happy tears?" He ran his fingers through his hair. "Or are you mad?"

"I'm not mad. I am just… stunned. I don't have the words. It's… my car."

"Let's sit inside." He walked around to the driver's side to open the door and stood, waiting.

I walked slowly around the wide front end, remembering all the work my father had to do to get the hood perfectly smooth. Smooth as butter, he would say. I reached out and ran my fingers along the glossy red paint, admiring the black twin stripes – they were just as straight now as they were back then. I never got to see how mangled it was after the accident, but now, I couldn't tell that it was even in an accident.

I sat in the driver's seat.

Chase gestured to the visor overhead. "I stole a picture of your dad from one of those albums you threw away. This way you can always have him with you."

I flipped it down to see a picture of my father sanding the passenger door of my car in our old garage, with my twelve-year old self grinning from ear to ear in the back seat. I kissed my fingers and touched them to his face in the photo. "He used to smile like that all the time when I was little."

Chase wiped my tears with his thumb and cradled my face in the palm of his hand. "All I wanted was for you to have a piece of him back."

"I cannot thank you enough for doing this. You have no idea how much this means to me. You have no idea how much you mean to me. I'm so incredibly lucky to have you."

"So, do you think you're up for a ride?"

"It has gas?" I sat straight up in my seat.

He grinned, reaching into his pocket. "You think I'd give you a car without gas?" He dangled the key before me.

I hesitated before putting the key into the ignition, remembering what happened the last time I started this car.

"Don't think about it. This is your new life. Most of the parts of this car are new, too. Everything is different now for you."

I nodded and took a deep breath as I pressed down on the clutch, and turned the key. It roared to a start and rumbled beneath me. I began laughing, as the tears continued to roll down my cheeks. I yanked my seatbelt on and revved the engine.

Chase jogged to the garage door opener.

"It sounds amazing! I can't believe you did this!" I shouted when he returned.

He swung himself into the passenger seat and clicked his seatbelt into place. "Let's go!"

In one swift motion, the car thundered out of the garage as my hands and feet worked together to shift seamlessly in and out of gears. With our windows rolled down, the cold winter air whipped against my tear-stained face, as my hair was being blown all around. I could see Chase watching me, his eyes intent on taking in every move I made. My eyes remained fixed ahead. I took the backroads so I would not have to slow down or stop at streetlights. I did not want to race, or to be reckless. All I wanted was open road – to feel wild and free.

I lost track of time until I felt Chase's hand on my leg. Finally, I began to slow down, working my way back down the gears. I pulled off the desolate road and killed the engine.

"So, what do you think?" Chase asked, already well-aware of the answer.

"I don't know if I'll ever get over the shock of this – you gave me my car back. I thought it was destroyed and gone forever."

"I'm glad I was able to see you drive it for the first time."

"For some people, I know driving is just a mindless task. Most just go through the motions in order to get from point A to point B. You know, they talk on the phone while they drive, or eat, or sing along to the radio while they're on autopilot. But for me, it's not mindless at all. It is the exact opposite. My mind is focused and clear when I am behind the wheel. It's like it captivates me and I can't think of anything else."

He twirled one of my curls around his finger. "I know. I can tell."

I shivered. "Ready to head back?"

"Yeah. I just need to lock up the shop and then you can take us home."

I started on my way back to the garage. "Do you want to sleep over my place tonight?"

"I would love to. You can park your shiny new car in the driveway."

"No, no. I won't take your family's spots. I'll park on the street."

"I'm not going to let my girlfriend park on the street."

"You keep calling me that."

"My girlfriend?"

"Yeah. I just… I didn't know…"

I saw him grinning from the corner of my eye. "When will you finally believe that I am in love with you and want to be with only you?"

I shrugged. "I don't know. You didn't tell me that you want to be with only me."

He laughed. "I thought that was implied when you tell someone you love them."

"Well, maybe I don't want you to imply. Maybe I want you to announce it. You know, shout it from the mountaintop or something."

"Baby, I just built a car for you. I think you're good."

When we arrived at the Brooks' home, I pulled up to the curb, parking on the street.

"You know I'll just move your car into the driveway myself."

"No, you won't." I flashed him a smile as I walked up the driveway.

"Let me grab a few things and I'll be over in a few," he called as he jogged to his front door.

I ran inside to quickly brush my teeth. I was about to change into comfier clothes, when something stopped me in my tracks. I sat on the edge of the bed, nervously awaiting Chase's arrival.

"Honey, I'm home!"

"Come in here," I called from my bedroom.

"Are you decent?" He poked his head through the cracked door.

"Yes, but I'm hoping you can change that." I pressed my lips against his, slipping my hands under his shirt to feel his warm skin. I stretched up onto my tippy toes to peel his shirt over his head.

"Whoa," he breathed, a hint of a smile on his face. "What are you doing?"

"I'm undressing you." I began unbuttoning his jeans.

"I can see that. But what are you doing?" He took my hands and held them inside his until I looked up at him.

"Can't a girl undress her boyfriend?"

He released my hands and pulled me in for another kiss. "I thought we could watch a movie on the couch with the Christmas tree lights on."

"You don't want to stay in here?"

"I'll do whatever you want to do. You just seemed in a hurry."

"I thought you would have wanted to."

"To do what? Have sex?"

I nodded, anxiously playing with the hem of my shirt. "Don't you want to?"

"Of course I want to have sex with you. I'm ridiculously attracted to you, and you're beyond sexy." He brushed my bottom lip with his thumb and gently kissed my mouth. "But I want to do it when the time is right for us. I don't want to be in a rush. What made you think I wanted to do it now?"

"I don't know. Shelly made a comment about it, and you just made this huge gesture with my car, and the tree."

He smiled as he sat on the corner of my bed. "So because I gave you something means you have to give me something in return?"

I slumped on the bed next to him, feeling foolish. "No."

"We will have sex when the time is right." He took my face into his hands. "And make no mistake – there will be no rush. I will take my time, and make love to every inch of your body."

"I'm looking forward to it," I whispered.

"So am I, baby." He kissed my forehead. "Can I put my shirt back on, now?"

I sighed dramatically. "Do you have to? I mean, that's such a good look."

He grinned as he tugged his shirt on over his head. "Ready for movie night?"

I nodded.

He stood and stepped into the hallway.

"Chase?"

He turned back and met his eyes with mine.

"I love you."

"I love you, Merritt. So much."

Chapter Seventeen: Christmas

"Merry! Chase! Wake up! Santa came!"

I rubbed my eyes and tried to put on my best excited face. "Okay, we're getting up now!"

Chase groaned from underneath his pillow.

Khloe put her tiny hands on his back and shook him. "Did you hear what I said? Santa came! There's a million presents downstairs! Let's go!"

"I'm up, I'm up. Go get mommy," he mumbled.

"I'll get him up. You go get your parents."

She nodded her head and left the room, like a tiny soldier reporting for duty. I heard her squeals, followed by multiple pairs of feet shuffling around down the hall. I glanced at the clock on Chase's nightstand, and wrapped my arms around his warm, sleepy body.

"What time is it?"

"Early bird catches the Christmas worm."

He peeked out from under his pillow and opened one eye, straining to see the numbers on the digital alarm clock. "Does that say five thirty?"

"It does." I giggled seeing his hair sticking up on all sides. "Let's go." I threw the covers off of us, smacked his ass, and hopped out of bed. I threw my sweatshirt on over my head, and checked the hallway to see if anyone was in the bathroom.

"When I get back here, I want to see you vertical."

Chase groaned, as I closed the door behind me.

Tanner suddenly stepped out into the hallway, his dark hair in the same disarray as Chase's was. He was shirtless, sporting nothing but a pair of loose-fitting boxers. His frame was thinner than his brother's, but his muscles were just as prominent.

"You going in?"

"Yeah, uh… but you can go ahead." I tried to act casual, as if my hair did not look like a giant squid monster was taking over my head.

"I just need to take a leak." He shuffled past me into the bathroom. "Then it's all yours."

I stood awkwardly in the hallway, while the sound of a firehose unleashed into the toilet. I did not hear a flush, nor did I hear the sound of the sink faucet. However, I did hear other gaseous sounds being expelled. I must have been making a face when he swung the door open, due to his amused grin.

"It better not smell in there," I warned, carefully stepping into the bathroom. I was immediately hit with an impressively foul odor. "Oh, God! Tanner! That smell can't be normal."

He chuckled. "Don't be dramatic."

"You couldn't have ripped that out there?! I rapidly began brushing my teeth, trying to breathe through my mouth.

Tanner laughed all the way into his bedroom.

"Real nice," Chase called into Tanner's room as he passed by. He leaned against the doorframe, watching me swish and spit into the sink. "I smell just as bad, you know."

I cringed at the thought. "Well, I'm not in any hurry to find out." I splashed water onto my face, and dried off on the towel hanging over the shower curtain.

"Hurry up, people!" Khloe screamed from the bottom of the stairs.

Chase, Tanner, and I trotted down the stairs. In the living room, Beverly and Tim were sitting under the tree, surrounded by presents. Chase sat on the nearby couch, and I sat on the floor in between his legs. His hand gently massaged my neck.

"Shit," Tanner said, plopping onto the couch. "Santa went all out this year, didn't he?"

"Tanner, it's Christmas. Why don't you watch your mouth? Just for today." Tim looked tired, his eyelids heavy and worn. His usual darkened skin tone was pale and greyish.

"Can we get this party started already?!"

We all winced in pain from Khloe's screech, but nobody told her to calm down. It was her last Christmas with her father, and we wanted her to enjoy it to the fullest.

She began tearing into the wrapping paper, opening one present after another. I asked Chase to get me a garbage bag, and began cleaning up all the scraps so the family did not have to worry about a mess afterwards. Khloe screamed as each present was revealed, even if it was a pack of underwear. Everything was equally exciting when it was from Santa Claus.

The family began exchanging gifts next, and I had an unexpected pile waiting to be opened next to me. To my surprise, one of the gifts was from Tanner. I decided to open that one first.

Inside the red gift bag was a pair of "New Car Smell" scented car fresheners, windshield cleaner, dashboard wipes, and a handmade coupon for one free carwash.

"Tanner, this is so thoughtful." I threw my arms around his neck. "Thank you so much."

"It's no big deal."

"Open my gift! Open mine!" Khloe jumped up and down, shoving her present into my lap. "I wrapped it myself."

"Really?" Tanner asked. "We couldn't tell."

I laughed. The present looked as if it got mauled by a bear. It was also covered in tape. When I opened it, tears instantly welled up in my eyes. Inside was a black velvet box holding a silver necklace; dangling from it was a heart engraved with a word: Sister.

"Do you like it?" she asked. "I got one, too!" She pulled out the silver chain hiding inside the collar of her pajama top.

"I love it." I blinked back the tears while I hugged her tightly.

"Now, you and Chase need to get married so we can really be sisters forever!"

Everyone burst into laughter.

I made eye contact with Chase. "Don't get any ideas."

He held his hands up innocently.

Tim and Beverly gave me a gift card to Bed, Bath and Beyond. "You can buy yourself anything else that you need for your apartment," Beverly said.

"You have done more than enough. You didn't need to do this." I hugged her and Tim simultaneously.

I was glad I did not listen to Chase when he told me not to worry about buying anything for his family. I handed a present to each family member: a cat-eared helmet to go with Khloe's new bike; a crystal picture frame for Beverly and Tim, displaying a picture I secretly arranged to take of their three kids; and a pair of boxing gloves for Tanner.

Tanner raised an eyebrow. "Boxing gloves?"

"It goes with Chase's gift." I prompted Chase to hand his brother the envelope.

Tanner held up the membership card from inside the envelope. "Is this the new MMA place that opened up?"

I nodded. "We figured you could hone your fighting skills."

"In a positive way," Chase added.

"This is awesome. Thanks, guys."

"What did you and Chase get for each other?" Khloe asked.

"Come here." I took Khloe's hand and led her to the window. "See that shiny red car outside? Chase built that for me."

Her eyes widened. "You made her a car?!"

"Yes, I did." Chase beamed proudly.

"I helped, too," Tanner reminded.

"Wow," she murmured. "You should definitely marry him, now, Merry. If someone gave me a car, I would marry them, too!"

The room erupted in laughter, again.

"What are you paying her to keep saying that?" Tanner asked Chase.

Chase tossed a pillow across the room at him.

"Pillow fight!" Khloe screamed, attacking Tanner with a pillow.

I noticed Tim whisper something to Beverly. She took his arm and helped him to stand. They walked out of the room, and she helped him up the stairs.

Chase leaned over, wrapping his arms around my shoulders. "He gets tired a lot, now."

I reached behind me to run my fingers through his velvety hair. "I'm sorry, baby."

"It's okay. I'm thankful that we have him with us today."

I nodded. "Me, too."

When Beverly returned, she began stuffing the rest of the scraps of wrapping paper into the garbage bag. "I'm going to start prepping everything for later."

"I will be in to help you, soon. I just need to give Chase his present."

She smiled. "Take your time."

Chase's eyebrows pushed together as I dragged him out the front door and up the stairs to my apartment. "I told you not to get me anything."

"Says the boy who built his girlfriend a car." I kept pulling his arm until we were standing in my bedroom. I pointed to the top drawer in my dresser. "Open it."

Besides the several wrapped presents sitting inside, the drawer was empty.

"Where did all of your clothes go?" he asked, pulling out the presents and setting them on the bed.

"I hung them in the closet. The top two drawers are yours."

He looked at me, confused. "What do you mean, mine?"

"I felt bad that I took the apartment that could have gone to you, and you made that comment about sleeping together more often… now you don't have to keep running to your house to get your things whenever you want to stay over. Open the rest of your presents."

He tore open the wrapping paper to reveal a toothbrush, deodorant, shampoo, and soap – in all of the brands that he used. His smile lit up his face.

"I mean, they don't compare to a car or anything…"

"Stop." He pulled me over to him and took my face into his large hands. "This gesture means more to me than any expensive gift. It means you want me to be around more."

"Yeah. I figured I needed someone here to kill the spiders once the spring comes."

He slapped my ass and pulled me against him. "You're real funny, you know that?" He slammed his lips into mine.

Since the first time we had kissed, each kiss was more passionate than the last. Our desire for each other was building up, like a smoking volcano preparing to erupt. It never seemed like the right time, especially not today with his family waiting for us to return. I wondered when our time would come.

Guess I'm taking another cold shower, I thought to myself.

Chapter Eighteen: The Sad Part

"What did Brody get you?"

"Well, it doesn't compare to a car, but he gave me a beautiful necklace."

"That's great, Shell. I can't wait to see it."

"Are you guys coming for New Year's or what? I need a head count."

"I don't think so. It all depends on how Tim is doing."

"Do you think he will make it until then?"

I sighed. "It's not looking good. The doctor recommended Hospice."

"Yikes. That must be so terrible, just sitting there waiting for death."

"It is terrible. My heart is breaking for them."

"How are you holding up going through all of this? You lost your dad, and now you have to lose Chase's dad."

"I'm trying to be strong for Chase. He's going to need it."

"You can't be strong for everyone, Xena. Don't bury it inside. You're allowed to cry and feel sad about it, too."

"I know."

"Chase won't feel like celebrating," Shelly admitted.

"No. I'm sorry. I know you were hoping we'd be there for the party."

"It's okay. I get it."

"There will be plenty of parties in the future. Don't you worry."

"I know, I know."

"Okay. Let me go see where he is. He was supposed to be over here by now. I'll talk to you later."

"Bye."

Christmas was over as quickly as it had arrived. Though it was the first Christmas without my father, I spent my first Christmas with a new family. The Brooks' house was filled with laughter and love. I felt sad, but focused my energy on enjoying the moment for them. If they could ignore the dark skies ahead, awaiting them beyond the holiday, then I could forget about my own storm that was behind me.

I looked at my phone. It was twenty minutes past the time Chase said he would be over. I peeked out the kitchen window to see who was home in the house below me. My car was the only one sitting out front. I slipped into my sneakers, and swung my jacket around my shoulders as I trotted down my stairs. Strangely, their door wasn't fully closed when I reached the front of the Brooks' house. I pushed it open and stepped inside.

"Hello? Your front door was open." I did not hear high-pitch squeals from Khloe; I did not hear the television; I did not hear anything. I searched the kitchen and dining room. Nothing. I climbed the stairs by twos. All of the bedroom doors were open, but no one was inside. Still, there was not a sound. I went back downstairs, as a sinking feeling swept over me.

There was no note. No explanation. None was needed. I knew what this meant. I ran out the door, and down the driveway. I swung myself into the driver's seat of my car and started the engine.

In what felt like seconds, I was running through the Emergency Room doors. I saw Tanner – the dark-haired boy with broken eyes sitting in a chair.

When his eyes rose up to meet mine, I did not have to ask. I did not say a word. I knelt on the floor in front of him, wrapped my arms around his shoulders, and he buried his face in my sweatshirt. I held him as he sobbed. Tim was gone.

He pulled away, reaching into his pocket to for his vibrating phone. "Yeah. She's here." He shoved the phone back into his pocket, and wiped his eyes quickly with his hands. "Mom is coming down with Khloe."

I felt the knot twist deeper into my stomach. I sat on the edge of the seat next to him, our eyes fixed on the double doors ahead. I didn't know what to expect, from either of them. I wondered how Chase was holding up.

Beverly emerged, carrying Khloe in her arms. "Thank you for coming," she said as she approached.

Khloe turned her head to see me. Her big eyes were red as she reached her arms out for me.

I held her tight, wishing I could absorb her pain into my own body. I was used to it. I could take it. She didn't have to go through this.

"Merry," she whispered with her head on my shoulders. "My daddy went to heaven, like yours did."

"I am so sorry, angel girl."

"Do you think he will see your dad? Do you think he knows what he looks like?"

I smiled as the tears spilled down my cheeks into her hair. "I think he will see my dad up there. I think they'll be good friends."

"I do, too." She sighed.

Beverly touched my arm. "Do you mind taking her for a little while? She shouldn't have to stay here for this part." One tear escaped her eye, which she swiftly swatted away. "I don't know who else to ask."

"Of course I will stay with her." I covered her hand with mine. "I will do anything you need me to do. Just say the word."

"Thank you. You can take the car seat out of my car." She kissed the top of my head. "I'm sorry to bother you."

I shook my head. "Don't be sorry. I'm glad I can be here to help."

Of all the times I wished I had died in the car accident, I suddenly found myself grateful to be here in this moment. Everything happens for a reason, Chase would say. I wanted to ask how he was doing, but I didn't. I knew I would see him eventually, but it killed me to drive away knowing he was mourning inside.

I watched as Beverly put her arm around Tanner, whispering into his ear. He shook his head at first, but reluctantly followed his mother back through the hospital doors. I carried Khloe out to the parking lot, and buckled her in her car seat.

When we got back to the house, I carried a sleeping Khloe up to my apartment. I laid her on my bed, and covered her with the blankets. Out in the living room, I paced, clutching my phone. I wanted to be there for him. I wanted to console him, though I knew well enough that there was nothing I could do. So I cleaned.

After an hour had passed, I heard my bedroom door crack open.

"Merry?"

I met Khloe in the hallway. "How did you sleep?"

She hugged my leg. "Your bed is so cozy."

I smiled and lowered myself to her eye-level. "How are you feeling?"

"Hungry. Do you have any snacks?"

"How about some pancakes? I can whip up a quick batch for you, if you're interested."

Her eyes widened. "I'm interested!"

I lifted her up and carried her to the kitchen counter, where I sat her upon. "Would you like to help?"

She nodded feverishly.

We began cracking eggs into the mixing bowl.

"Where do you go when you die?" Khloe's question broke into my thoughts. I wanted to keep conversation light, but I would not ignore her questions.

"To Heaven."

"How do you know?"

"Well, I don't really know for sure. But that's what everybody says happens."

"How do they know?"

"I don't think anybody really knows how it all works. The only people who know are the ones who are already there."

"I wonder what it's like."

"Heaven?"

"When you die."

I wished I had known what Beverly had already told Khloe about death. It was hard thinking of the right things to say on the spot.

"Okay, now we need to give this a good mixing." I handed her the whisk. "You can do the honors."

Her tiny hand wrapped around the handle, as I held the bowl in place. Her furrowed eyebrows told me our conversation was not over.

"Why did your dad die?"

I took a deep breath. "Uh… well… he was sick."

"Like my dad?"

"He didn't have cancer. He was a different kind of sick."

"Chase told me that your dad was sick in his brain."

I nodded in agreement. "He was."

"What happened to him when he died?"

"Pancakes are ready for pouring! Now, be very careful not to touch this pan. It will get very hot."

"Can I help you flip them?"

"Of course." I poured the first pancake onto the pan, and handed her the spatula. "We have to wait until we see little bubbles popping on the pancake. That's how we know it's time to flip it over."

"Do you feel pain when you die?"

"I don't think so. I don't think you even realize you're dying. I think it just happens. Like you're falling asleep."

"Mommy said you almost died. In your car accident."

I nodded. "But someone saved me and brought me to the hospital."

"We brought daddy to the hospital. But nobody saved him."

I touched her rosy cheek. "Sometimes when you have cancer, you can't be saved."

"Look! The bubbles are popping! Let's flip it over!"

I blinked back the tears that had welled up into my eyes. I guided the spatula while Khloe flipped the pancake onto the other side, squealing in delight.

"I did it!"

"Great job, babe! Want to set the table for us?"

She nodded. "You let me do all the cool grown-up stuff. That's why I love you so much."

I smiled and hugged her tightly before setting her down on the floor. "I love you so much. Here are the plates. Forks are in this drawer. Napkins are on the table."

I poured the next pancakes onto the pan, and pulled my phone out of my back pocket. No new text messages. I sighed, and set it on the counter.

When we sat down to eat, there was a knock at the front door. We both jumped up to see who it was.

"Tanner!" Khloe jumped into his arms. "We made pancakes! Do you want some?"

My heart sank.

"Nah. I'm not hungry."

"Are you guys all back?" I asked.

"Yeah. Mom said to come get Khloe." His eyes did not look at me when he spoke.

"We were just about to eat. I can bring her over when she's done, if that's okay?"

"Sure." He set Khloe down in front of me. "See you soon, squirt."

Khloe ran back inside.

"Tanner?" I called to him as he trotted down the stairs. "Is Chase home, too?"

"He said he was taking a nap."

I nodded as I watched him disappear around the front of the house.

"Hurry up, Merry! Your pancakes are getting cold."

I closed the door and returned to the table. Again, I checked my phone. No new messages.

We finished eating in silence. I was grateful to not have to answer any more questions about death.

"Can I help you wash the dishes?" Khloe asked as we cleaned off the table.

"I'll do them later. Thanks for offering, though. You have such great manners."

She smiled so big, I could see every tooth in her mouth. Her smile was contagious, and I felt my cheeks pushing up, too.

"Let's get you home."

She held my hand with her tiny human fingers as we walked up to the front door of her house. She hesitated before reaching her hand out to the doorknob.

"Will daddy be home?" Her wide eyes blinked up at me.

I knelt down in front of her. "No, babe. He stayed at the hospital."

"When will I see him again?"

My heart shattered. "Probably in a few days, at the funeral."

She nodded, her eyebrows furrowed again.

"We don't have to go inside yet if you're not ready. You tell me what you want to do."

She squared her shoulders, and turned to face the door. "I'm ready."

I pushed open the door and we stepped inside, together.

"Is that you, my Kokomo?" Beverly appeared from the kitchen.

Khloe ran to her and hugged her leg. "I helped Merry make pancakes!"

"Wow. I bet they were delicious."

"They were. I flipped them and everything."

Beverly looked at me with a tired, grateful expression. "Thank you so much for watching her."

I waved my hand. "It was my pleasure. I can watch her any time you need me."

"Khlo, why don't you go up to your room to play? I'll be up in a few minutes."

"Bye, Merry!" She waved her tiny wave, and ran up the stairs.

Beverly rubbed her eyes. "I really appreciate your help."

"I mean it – I will watch her any time. She had some questions. I wasn't sure how to answer them."

She laughed. "I never know the right answers to her billions of questions, either."

I reached out and squeezed her arm. "Do you need me to do anything? I can cook, or clean. Do you need groceries?"

Beverly shook her head. "No. You've done enough. Thank you, Merritt." She looked at the stairs. "Chase is laying down. You can go up, if you'd like. I'm sure he would love to see you."

I paused before speaking. "No. Let him sleep. I'm sure he'll call me later."

"Just give him some time. I think he's going to take this the hardest."

I nodded in agreement. Tanner would bury it. Khloe was young and resilient. But Chase – he would go through every single emotion like someone trying to run through wet cement. "I wish there was something I could do."

Beverly raised her hand to my cheek. "Having you by his side is all he needs."

"And what about you? What do you need?"

Her voice waivered as she answered. "It will take time."

I mustered up a smile before turning to leave. I closed the door behind me, and jogged up the stairs to my apartment. I knew I had to wait it out, and let Chase come to me when he felt ready. All I wanted to do was hold him while he slept.

I sat on my couch and called Shelly.

"I was just about to call you," she answered.

"Oh, yeah? What for?"

"I've got some gift cards that are burning a hole in my wallet. Want to take a ride to the mall with me?"

"No. I called to tell you that Tim… he passed away this morning."

"Oh, Merritt. I am so sorry. We were just talking about it this morning. How awful."

"I know."

"It's good that he was able to make it through Christmas."

"Yeah."

"How is Chase doing?"

"I don't know, actually."

"What do you mean?"

"Well, his mom asked me to watch Khloe while they were at the hospital. I never saw him. I hung out with Khloe for a couple hours until they were back. Tanner came to get her."

"Tanner? You mean Chase didn't come by when he got back?"

"No. His mom said he was laying down."

Shelly was quiet for a moment. "He's tired, and heart-broken. He just needs some time alone to process everything."

"I know. I just wish I could be there for him. It sucks sitting here, waiting."

"You know, you do have another option."

"Like what?"

"You pushed everyone away when you lost your dad. Who was the only person you let near you, besides me?"

"Chase didn't exactly give me a choice."

"Right."

I sat quietly, remembering all the times Chase showed up with food, and insisted on driving me places.

"Don't let him isolate himself. That will only make things worse. Go over there and take care of him."

"Even if he doesn't want me there?"

"If he listened to you every time you told him to go away, you wouldn't be where you are right now."

"You're right."

"I always am! Now, go!"

"Thanks, Shell."

"Oh! I have a candy striper costume, if you want to borrow it. That would definitely help him out of his funk."

"I don't really think that would go over too well, with him living with his mother and four-year old sister."

"Oh, yeah. Forgot about that part."

"Bye, Shell."

I sat on my couch, unsure. I thought about all the casseroles, pies, and fruit baskets people sent me the first few days following my father's death; I thought about all the arrangements I had to make for his funeral, and the phone calls to let people know about his service; I thought about Beverly, knowing all too well that she would not ask her sons for help. I began making a mental list of all the things that needed to be done, and before I could talk myself out of it, I was out the door.

Chapter Nineteen: My Turn

I rang the bell with my elbow, both hands full.

"Merritt, what is all this?"

"These bags need to be refrigerated. Careful, this is the one that has the eggs." I ran back out to my car to grab the remaining bags.

Beverly and Khloe were standing in the doorway of their house.

"Merry brought pizza!" Khloe exclaimed as I walked back up their driveway.

Tanner appeared in the entryway, ready to take the box out of my hands. "Sweet. I'm starving."

"Merritt," Beverly followed me into the kitchen. "You didn't have to do all of this. This is too much."

Without stopping, I began loading the groceries onto the island in the middle of her kitchen. "Don't worry about it. It was nothing."

"This is not nothing. What was the total? I will give you the money for everything."

"I refuse to take your money. Sit and have a slice with your kids. I bet you haven't eaten anything all day."

"It does smell good." She glanced at Khloe and Tanner in the dining room.

"After you're done, I have all the numbers we need to start making the arrangements. The place that did my father's service was very reasonably priced – well, you were there, you saw it. I can call, and you can call any of your family members and friends that need to be notified once we have the dates and times. Divide and conquer, and we'll have it all done in no time."

Beverly gently took the gallon of milk out of my hands, and placed it down on the island beside us. Silent tears were streaming down her cheeks, as she pulled me into her embrace. I knew she would not want her kids to know that she was crying, so I said nothing.

"Chase, Look! Merry brought pizza!" Khloe yelled from the dining room.

In the doorway to the kitchen, Chase's bloodshot eyes met with mine. I held my finger to my lips to prevent him from saying anything. I wanted to run to him, but Beverly needed to let it out, and I would not let go of her until she loosened her hold on me first. He surveyed the grocery bags scattered on the floor before making his way into the dining room.

After several minutes, Beverly released me and took a step back. She wiped her eyes with the backs of her hands, and proceeded to put the remaining groceries away. I handed her a paper towel, and she quickly blew her nose.

"Let's go have a bite to eat before we get started," she quietly suggested.

I nodded. My stomach was in a giant knot as I approached the table in the dining room and took the chair next to Chase.

"Thanks for bringing all of this," he muttered without looking at me.

"Are you having a slice?" I asked, motioning to his empty plate.

He shook his head. "Not hungry."

"Chase, you haven't eaten anything since dinner last night. You need to eat something," Beverly said, trying to mask the worry in her voice.

"I'll eat when I feel hungry." He stood. Without saying another word, he walked out of the room.

I listened to his slow footsteps on the stairs, and the closing of his bedroom door. I tried to ignore the fact that Tanner, Khloe, and Beverly were all looking at me with the same expression.

"He's just tired," Beverly tried.

"This isn't something he can just sleep off," Tanner snapped. "Dad's gone, and the sooner he comes to terms with that, the better off he'll be." He pushed his chair back from the table and took his plate into the living room.

"Chase doesn't know that daddy died?" Khloe asked, looking confused.

"He does, baby. He's just very sad about it." Beverly ran her fingers through her hair. "Why don't you go upstairs, Merritt? See if he'll talk to you. Maybe you can get him to eat something."

I nodded. "I'll try. We can get the phone calls started when I come back down."

She reached across the table and squeezed my hand. "Thank you, Merritt."

"Can I come with you?" Khloe asked, jumping up from her seat when I stood.

"Let her go alone. Why don't we go ask Tanner to put a movie on?"

"I hope we can watch Moana!" Khloe took her mother's hand as she led her into the living room. "Daddy loved watching Moana."

My heart wrenched with every reminder Khloe made. Upstairs, I stood outside Chase's bedroom door, hesitant to knock. I took a deep breath. "Chase, it's me. Can I come in?"

"Doors open." His voice was muffled.

I closed the door behind me as I entered the darkened room. I stepped over the minefield of tissues, making my way to his bed. I slipped under the covers next to him, and wrapped my arm around his midsection, planting small kisses along the back of his neck. His body remained still.

"We don't have to talk if you don't want to."

"Good," he mumbled. "I have nothing to say."

"You don't need to say anything. I just want to lie here with you."

He exhaled, and I felt his body finally relax. His breathing soon became steady. I laid there, nuzzled against his broad back, trying to pour all of my strength into him while he slept. After some time had passed, I backed out of the bed. Quietly, I picked up all of the tissues that were strewn about the floor, and tiptoed into the hallway.

Tanner appeared at the top of the stairs, on his way to his own bedroom. He looked down at the pile of used tissues in my arms.

"Gross."

I rolled my eyes. "Your mother doesn't need to hear your shit, and neither does Khloe. So you two need to man up, quick." I pushed past him to get to the bathroom and dumped the tissues into the garbage before heading downstairs. I didn't look back to see his reaction.

Beverly was sitting at the dining room table, an opened address book in front of her. She stared at it, with her hands in her lap.

I sat down beside her. "Where's Khloe?"

"She fell asleep watching Moana. I'm trying to get up the nerve to make the first call."

I placed my hand on her shoulder. "I know how hard it is to say the words. I promise it gets easier as you go."

"I don't know how you did this all by yourself."

"I did everything by myself growing up. It was normal for me."

She turned to face me. "I don't ever want you to feel alone again. You are a part of our family, and we will always be here for you."

I smiled. "The same goes for you, too. I'm always here whenever you guys need me."

"I guess I need to get started." She flipped through the pages aimlessly. "I don't know who to call first."

"Start with the people closest to you. Tim's parents, your parents, or any brothers or sisters he might have."

"That's easy. Both of our parents passed away a long time ago, and we don't have any siblings. It was really just the five of us for so long."

Tears welled up in her eyes as she accepted the fact that their family was no longer a party of five.

"That's okay. You guys will be the fearless foursome, now."

She smiled as a tear rolled down her cheek. "I like that."

"But you make us five, again." Tanner sat down across from us at the table. "So, who are we calling?"

I smiled at him, thankful that he was able to put everything aside to help his mother.

"Well, I guess I should start with Steve and Howard. Then the Danielsons, next door."

"Can I ask what Tim's wishes were, for the funeral service?"

"He wanted to be cremated," Tanner replied quietly.

"We will have a wake with the viewing. We felt like it would be best for Khloe to see him one last time."

I nodded in agreement. "And then the cremation. You'll be keeping his ashes?"

They both nodded.

"Why don't you start there? This way, when you call people, you have the dates and times ready for them."

"Good idea," Beverly said. Her hand shook as she picked up her phone to dial.

Tanner and I began making a list of people to call. While Beverly was on the phone, Khloe stumbled out of the living room.

"Merry, you're still here." She crawled into my lap.

"How was Moana?" I kissed her head as I wrapped my arms around her tiny body.

"I felt sad watching it without daddy."

"Me, too," Tanner agreed.

"That will happen sometimes," I said, rocking her gently in my arms. "You will remember all of the fun times you had together, and that can make you sad because you miss him. It's okay to feel sad and miss him."

"Do you know what I do when I get sad?" she asked. "I imagine him having fun with your dad in Heaven. I think he's having a good time up there."

Tanner's gaze lowered to his lap.

"I think that's a great thing to imagine." I squeezed her extra tight.

Chase emerged from his bedroom, only to go to the bathroom. He returned to his room, and closed the door behind him.

"Why won't he come down with us?" Khloe asked, sadness in her voice.

"You know how sad you felt watching Moana? Chase feels that sadness, too. Sometimes, sadness makes you very tired. My dad was so sad once that he used to sleep all day and all night."

"Why was he so sad?" she asked.

"My mom moved very far away, and we couldn't see her anymore. He loved her so much, and he missed her so much, that he was sad without her."

"Why did she move away?"

I shrugged my shoulders, anticipating that question. "I don't know. She wasn't a very good mom, like yours is. Your mommy would never leave you guys behind."

"No, she wouldn't," Beverly stated, sitting back down at the table.

Khloe curled up into her lap.

"Did I hear Chase upstairs?" she asked.

"Yup. Just to take a piss, and then locked himself in his room again," Tanner replied bluntly.

"I'm going to bring him some pizza." I stood and pushed my chair in. "I'll be back down in a little while."

"Don't worry about me," Beverly waved. "Focus on getting him to eat something."

I nodded as I went into the kitchen. I slapped a slice of pizza onto a paper dish, and grabbed a water bottle out of the fridge. I knocked on his bedroom door before entering, and let myself in.

"I brought you pizza and water. I'm going to leave it on your nightstand for when you get hungry."

"I'm not hungry." His voice was muffled as it was before.

"I know. But you will be later, so it's here." I sat on the edge of the bed, lightly rubbing his back that was facing me. "Can I get you anything else?"

I waited in his silence. I leaned over and kissed his cheek. It was wet. I slid under the covers once more, and pressed myself against him as tightly as I could.

"You don't have to stay here," he muttered.

"I know I don't have to. I'm staying until you tell me to leave."

To that, he did not reply.

"Do you want me to go?" I asked.

"No."

"Turn around, Chase. Look at me."

Slowly, he turned over. We laid facing each other, as I caressed his face. "You were there for me while I was going through the worst time. Now, I'm going to be here for you during your worst time. So you can keep trying to push me away, but I'm not going anywhere." I might not be as charming as you were, but I can be just as persistent.

I saw the tiniest hint of a smirk appear on his face. "I am pretty charming."

"Of course that's what you heard." I rolled my eyes.

"I don't want to eat; I don't want to talk about my feelings; and I don't want to make phone calls to random people to tell them that my father died."

"Fine. So what do you want then?"

"I want to lay here, staring at your beautiful face, until I fall asleep."

"That we can do."

We stared into each other's eyes for a small while. I watched the tears fill up behind his eyelids, and I watched him blink them away, like waves rushing onto the sand only to return just as quickly back to the ocean.

Daylight turned to moonlight, and still we laid.

"I have something for you," Chase's voice broke the silence in the darkened room around midnight.

"You do?"

"It's from my father."

"Oh. What is it?"

He stretched past me and switched his lamp on. Now sitting up, he reached into the pocket of his sweatpants and pulled out a folded piece of white paper.

I sat up, too.

He ran his fingers through his hair. He was nervous. "He asked me to give it to you before he died."

I took the paper from him, and unfolded it, and began to read.

Chapter Twenty: The Letter

Dear Merritt,

I have wanted to tell you this for quite some time, but I never knew how to say it. Now that I've got limited time, I'm afraid I won't get the chance. I hope you can forgive me for doing this in a letter.

As a parent, all you want in life is to see your children happy. When I saw the way Chase lit up when he was with you, I felt I could leave in peace knowing that he had you. It's funny to think how you were right under each other's noses all along. Sometimes, you're not ready to meet someone until you reach a certain point in your life. It's like the universe was preparing you both for the exact moment when your worlds would finally collide.

The night of your father's wake, we had already found out about my cancer. I knew Chase was thinking about how he would one day be in your shoes, at my funeral. He was hurting for you. When he realized how much you had to drink, he wanted to get you out of there, and take you home; in hindsight, I wish that he had. Perhaps he would have gotten you home safely that night. But you left before anyone could stop you. He insisted on following you.

Beverly and I were only in the car for a few minutes when he called us for help. I turned around, and got to you as quickly as I could. You were stuck, and Chase was beside himself. He couldn't manage to get you out before the flames engulfed the front end of the car. Afraid the car would explode, I pulled on you as hard as I possibly could. I'm afraid I caused your shoulder more damage than you should have had, and for that I am sorry. But I was determined to get you out of there – determined not to let this sweet, young girl die right before my son's eyes. If I couldn't be saved from what fate had in store for me, at least I could save you.

I know how much Chase hates keeping this secret from you. He said that you didn't want to know. Please don't be angry with him. I know what it means if you're reading this letter, and he needs you right now. They all will need you. Your immeasurable strength is comforting to me. I know they will be okay, in time. And so will you, Merritt. I would give anything to have a second chance at life – to watch my family grow up, to see where they will go in their lives, to help them with anything they need. You get to do that now. Promise me you will help them – and let them help you, too. You deserve it.

All My Love – Tim

The tears poured down my face as the last piece of the puzzle was put into place. I squeezed my eyes shut, trying to remember the sound of the voice that I heard while I was trapped in the car. It was a voice I would never hear again.

I looked up at Chase. He looked blurry through the waterfall of tears.

"Are you mad?" he asked.

All I could do was shake my head. There were no words offering themselves up for me to say.

"I wanted to tell you. But the first day I drove you to therapy, you blurted out that you wished you had died in the accident. I knew you would want nothing to do with me if I told you that I was responsible for you getting saved."

"This is why you believe everything happens for a reason?"

"If my dad never got sick, I wouldn't have been home from California. I wouldn't have been at your dad's funeral. I wouldn't have been there to follow you." He choked back the tears as he took my hands into his. "You would have died in that wreck, and I would never have gotten the chance to tell you how much I love you."

Everything made sense, now. A strange sense of relief washed over me as I finally got the closure I didn't realize I needed. The tears forced themselves out, wave after wave, as I sat in disbelief on Chase's bed.

"What are you thinking right now?" he asked, nervously.

"You... you saved me. Your dad saved me. I'll never be able to thank him."

"I thanked him plenty, trust me." Chase wiped the tears from my cheek with his thumb. "I wish you could have seen him. I don't know how he got you out of there, Merritt. I tried with all of my might. It's a memory my mother and I will always carry with us. He was heroic."

"All I remember are the clips from my dreams, and they were horrifying. He was so brave to do that." I sat up after a moment. "I have to tell Shelly."

Chase shook his head. "She already knows."

My jaw dropped open. "What?"

"My dad took you to the hospital. My mom and I went back to the funeral home to get Shelly. We waited in the hospital together. Then, we found out that you were in a coma. She was terrified. She really beat herself up for letting you leave."

"Who else knows?"

"No one. Well, I'm sure she told Brody. Oh, and Tanner knows."

I nodded, falling silent again. I couldn't pick one clear thought out of my head as a million more questions raced through my mind.

"Do you want to lie down?" Chase motioned to my favorite spot in his arms.

I curled up inside his embrace. Facing me, he pulled the covers around us. "I know it's noisy in there," he said, kissing my forehead. "Do you have any other questions you want to ask?"

I sighed. "No. Not now, anyway. I don't want to take the focus off of you."

"I don't mind the distraction, honestly."

I couldn't help but smile.

"What?"

"Ever since you came into my life, you have taken my mind off of all the bad things that happened. Now, the roles have reversed."

His grin illuminated the dim room.

"There's my smile." I took hold of his face and kissed his lips. "I hate it when you're sad."

"Even though I knew this day would come, I don't think it makes it hurt any less."

"No. I don't imagine it would."

"Thank you for helping my mom. That meant the world to me."

"She could use your help, too. She's worried about you."

"I'm not ready to be around them yet. It's too hard, seeing one less family member that should still be here with us."

"I get it."

"Between your accident, and his cancer, all I can think about is how brief the good moments are. They can be ripped away from you at any time – with or without warning... and there's nothing we can do."

I ran my fingers through his hair. "I know. It's scary. I've focused on the bad things for so long. It makes me not trust the good moments, like I'm waiting for the rug to be pulled out from underneath me."

"I don't want it to be pulled out from under us. I want to be with you for a very, very long time."

"Ditto, babe."

He yawned.

"Want me to shut the light?"

"No. Don't. I'm not done looking at you yet."

We laid there until Chase's eyelids grew heavy. Mine were not closing any time soon. It was too busy in my mind. I was going over every detail that I could remember from the night of my father's funeral. I tried willing my mind to remember Chase and his father, but all I could see were the smoke and flames.

Chase was right – life is short. Such a common statement, yet only now did I understand its true meaning. I had spent so much of my life focusing on my sick father; so much time wallowing in my own despair; so much time looking back on the things I could not change. Happiness was sleeping just inches away from me, now. I felt a sense of urgency taking over. I had wasted enough time. I needed to make a change, a vow to myself, that I would be better – more present – for the people in my life. I owed it to Tim.

The hours passed, and soon the sun began streaming through the windows in the Brooks' house. I crept downstairs while everyone was still asleep. As quietly as I could manage, I began making breakfast: pancakes, eggs, and bacon. I wondered how Beverly slept, if at all.

Not before long, footsteps overhead signaled the family was awakening.

"I smell pancakes!" Khloe shouted from the top of the stairs.

"I smell bacon," Chase shouted back. "I'll race ya to the kitchen!"

I breathed a sigh of relief. Chase had emerged from his room in better spirits, if only for the sake of his family.

Both he and Khloe simultaneously slid into the kitchen. Khloe was the first to reach me, as she crashed into my leg.

"I won! I won!"

Chase pretended to run after her, which sent her flailing around the island, and into the dining room.

"I could get used to this sight." I felt his hands on my waist and I flipped the last pancake onto the pan.

I smiled, leaning into his touch. "What sight is that?"

"You, making breakfast in my pajamas."

"They're a tad big on me," I laughed. "Okay, go sit. Everything is done."

He turned me around to face him. "Thank you for everything. I love you so much."

I looked into his eyes, as I had once tried so hard not to do. "I love you," I replied, reaching up on my toes to meet his lips.

"Alright, alright. You're going to ruin my appetite," Tanner grumbled as he lumbered into the kitchen.

"That would be a shame." I walked past him with the heaping plate of pancakes in one hand, and the bacon in another.

"Mommy's not up yet," Khloe stated.

I set the plates down on the table in front of her. "Don't worry. She's tired. Let her rest."

"But she's always up before we are." Her eyes were glued to the stairs just outside the dining room.

Chase took his usual chair beside her. "She was up really late last night."

Her eyes were wide. "Why?"

"She was on the phone with our neighbors next door." He gestured to the left with his thumb.

I watched as Tanner loaded his plate with everything I had laid out on the table. He remained standing, pouring syrup over it all.

"That's gross." Khloe scrunched her nose up in disgust.

"You're gross," he retorted.

"Am not." She stuck her tongue out at him.

He tousled her hair before walking out of the room.

"Hey, where are you going?" she called after him.

"To watch TV," he called back.

"Why is nobody having a family breakfast today?" her tiny voice asked.

"Why don't we play a game?" I suggested.

"What kind of game?"

"When my mom moved away, I was really sad for a while. I would sit at the table for dinner, and stare at her empty seat where she always used to sit. One night, my dad sat down with me and asked me what I would want to talk to her about if she was there. I came up with all these different conversations that we could have. It was fun, and it helped me not to miss her so much. Do you think you would want to try that?"

Her eyes lit up. "Let's pretend both of our dads are here!"

"Okay. What would you say first?"

"I would say, Hi Mister – wait, what's your dad's name?"

Chase stifled a laugh.

"Robert. His friends all called him Rob."

"Okay. Hi Mister Rob. I'm Khloe. This is my brother, Chase." She looked at Chase, clearly waiting for him to introduce himself.

"Oh. Sorry. Hi, sir. I'm Chase."

It was my turn to stifle a laugh.

"What is it like up in Heaven?" she asked her next bold question.

We all waited in silence.

"He said it's beautiful," Khloe reported. "Everything is white and puffy in the clouds, and there's always music playing."

"Sounds awesome," I replied. "Did he say if he's hanging out with your dad a lot?"

"Daddy is right there." She pointed to his seat at the table. "He says they play poker and go bowling together."

I noticed Chase kept glancing at the doorway. I stood and began making a small plate of food for Beverly. I slipped out while Khloe was in deep conversation with her father. Upstairs, Beverly's door was closed. I imagined last night was extremely difficult, as it was the first night without her husband. I took a deep breath before knocking lightly on the door.

"Beverly? It's Merritt. I brought some breakfast up for you, if you're hungry."

I listened for a moment, and cracked the door open when I didn't hear a response. When I looked inside, I saw tissues strewn about the floor, much like the pile Chase had in his room the day before. Beverly, awake, was sitting up in bed with red eyes.

"Oh, Beverly." I closed the door behind me and set her plate down on her nightstand.

"Every time I tell myself that I'm going to stop crying, more tears keep pouring out." She wiped her nose with a tissue. "Do your tear ducts ever run dry?"

I sat on the bed next to her and shook my head. "No. I'm afraid they don't."

She looked down at the plate of food. "You're so good, Merritt. Thank you so much for taking care of us through all this. I don't know what I'd do without you here." Tears streamed down her cheeks again. "Tim and I were partners. I always thought we would have each other."

I let a tear escape my eye. "I'm so sorry. I know how badly it sucks – it's like you had this whole vision of what life would be like, and now you have to start from scratch and figure out how you're going to go on with your life in this new way."

She nodded feverishly. "Exactly. Everything was going just fine – then the cancer ruined everything. It wasn't supposed to be like this! We had a plan."

I hugged her as she sobbed. "I know. We make all these plans, and for what? Life takes us for its own ride." I handed her another tissue.

"How are the kids?"

"They're okay. Chase is feeling better today. Tanner is his moody self. I taught Khloe a new game she can play where she talks to Tim as if he is still there. I hope you don't mind that. It won't last for long."

She wiped her eyes. "I think that's a great idea for her. Thank you."

"You don't have to keep thanking me. I'm glad to be here." I paused a moment. "Speaking of being here… I read Tim's letter last night."

She nodded. "I figured it was only a matter of time before Chase gave it to you. How do you feel about it?"

"I'm shocked, really. I can't believe it was you guys who got me out of there."

"I was so scared that Tim wasn't going to be able to pull you out in time."

"I'm so lucky that he did." I meant the words as I said them aloud for the first time.

She held my face against her palm. "You have been through so much. It's time you start living a happy life."

"I think that life has already started."

Chapter Twenty-one: No Strings Attached

The next couple of days were tough to get through. Each member of the Brooks family had his and her ups and downs as they experienced Tim's two-day wake. Today would be the final day – his funeral – and it would undoubtedly be the hardest. Tensions were running high for all of us, and I was looking forward to getting today over with. We were desperate for a distraction from our lives. We needed some relief from the sadness.

After a shower, I stared into my closet searching for something appropriate to wear. I played with the belt on my robe while I put outfit possibilities together in my head. Nothing ever seemed right when picking out an outfit for a funeral.

Minutes later, Chase emerged from my bathroom, the towel sitting loosely around his waist. Instinctually, my eyes followed him as he made his way to the bed where his suit was laid out. It seemed like years had passed since we kissed. Our relationship had begun amidst a difficult time, and we had not gotten the real beginning that couples normally get. Ever since reading Tim's letter, I felt like there was a giant hourglass looming over us, as if our time together could run out at any moment. Even though we spent all of our time together, it seemed like there was never enough time spent truly enjoying the moments that we had.

"Take a picture. It'll last longer," Chase teased, walking towards me.

I ran my hands down his smooth chest. It was impossible to stand this close to him, in nothing but a towel, and not touch him. My hands longed to feel his skin. Every fiber of my being was crying out for his body. I stretched up to reach his mouth and pressed my lips against his. My tongue parted his lips, playfully calling out its partner. I tugged on his towel, but he intercepted.

"What are you doing?" he murmured.

"What we should have been doing all along." I ran my fingers through his damp hair and pulled him in for another passionate kiss.

"Are you sure?" His eyes were staring into mine the way one stares at a red light that is about to change, impatiently begging for it to turn green.

"I've never been more sure. We need to enjoy what we have, while we have it. I don't want to waste another second with you."

With that, he pulled on the ends of my belt, opening my robe and sliding it off my shoulders. I tore off the towel from around his waist, and pressed myself against him as we kissed. In the doorway of my closet, we stood before each other completely naked for the first time. My mind flashed to how terrified I was to move along the rim of the Grand Canyon years ago; now, I was base-jumping off the cliff.

I left his lips, and made a trail of kisses down to his stomach. Though I could have marveled over his perfectly chiseled abs for hours, I kept going downward. Before anything or anyone could interrupt us, I took him into my mouth. His hand rested on the back of my neck while I massaged him with my tongue, gliding him in and out from between my lips. I glanced up to see his head leaning back against the doorframe, eyes closed and mouth open, breathing more quickly each time I swirled my tongue around him. Pulsating as he was, I could tell that he would not last long. He felt it, too, and gently pulled me up to my feet after only a few minutes.

"I don't want to stop," I whimpered as he began kissing my neck.

"I need you to." Slowly, he knelt down in front of me, his hands roaming through places that they had not yet been. He took one of my legs and swung it over his shoulder. I reached back to hold onto the end of my dresser for support as soon as I felt his warm tongue on me. It was a feeling nobody had ever made me feel before. No one else could – no one else was him. I pushed his head further in between my legs. With both of his hands gripping my ass, his licks became stronger as he rubbed his tongue against me. I moaned and moved my hips in time with his rhythm.

The intensity grew, and soon that wonderful feeling began to creep up. That was when Chase retracted his tongue, and kissed his way up my body.

"Why do you keep stopping?!"

He grinned, walking me backwards to the bed. "I'm not finished with you yet."

"Good because I am just getting started with you." I pointed to the bed. "Lay down."

"Yes, ma.am." His eyes followed me as I walked around the bed to my nightstand.

I pulled an unopened box of condoms out of the drawer, and silently thanked Shelly for including it in my Christmas gift as I tore into it. I ripped one of the squares off the strip, and tossed the wrapper onto the floor as I climbed on top of Chase. I rolled the condom onto him, and with our eyes fixated on each other, I guided him inside of me.

We let out simultaneous sighs as our bodies converged. All of our fears and pent up frustrations were released in that moment. For so long, we had shared in each other's pain, and now we could finally share in each other's ecstasy.

We moved in sync, as if we had already been together like this many times before. His hands gripped my waist, pushing and pulling me back and forth onto him. Feeling his impressive presence inside me, I arched my back and held onto his thighs, wanting him deeper with every thrust. Sweat began to form on my skin.

"You look fucking incredible up there."

"You should see my view." I caressed his beautiful face and ran my fingers down his chest, onto his cubed abdominals that stretched and contracted each time we merged. Every muscle in his body rippled with every movement he made. He was a god.

Being on top of Chase Brooks was something I could not have imagined. I felt like an untamed horse running through the wild; like I had broken free of the reins that were holding me back for so long. With him, I could let myself go. I had never felt this with anyone before – to look into his eyes with complete transparency and vulnerability.

The surge of passion between us began to heighten, and my hips began to move faster. I reached for the headboard on my bed for leverage. I tried to prolong it, wanting this moment to last as long as it possibly could, but it felt too good not to give in.

"Oh my God... Chase..." I closed my eyes as my whole body shook. Our rocking slowed while Chase sat up, still inside of me, and gently kissed around my neck and chest. Every part of me tingled, all the way down to my toes, while I tried to catch my breath.

Suddenly, he flipped me onto my back and took over control on top of me. I wrapped my arms and legs around his body and drew him in as close as I could. I outlined his ear with my tongue, continuing down to his neck. Every sense was awakened, and I wanted to see, smell, touch and taste him all at the same time. His groans got louder each time he plunged into me. Reaching down to grab two handfuls of his ass, I drove him deeper inside.

"You feel so fucking good," he breathed.

Our pace got faster, until our bodies were dripping with sweat. He closed his eyes and gripped my thigh tighter as he called out with his final thrust. Our movements slowed to a stop, and we laid panting wrapped up in each other's arms.

"That was unbelievable," he said, out of breath.

"Why haven't we been doing this all along?"

He grinned. "It was worth the wait." Leaning in for a kiss, he stroked my cheek with his thumb. "I love you more than you will ever know, Merritt."

"I love you, Chase. So, so much."

I wanted to stay there in bed with him, though I knew time was ticking. I wiped my forehead with the back of my hand. "I think I need another shower."

"If you wait until tonight, maybe I'll join you." He winked and made his way back into the bathroom. I watched him walk away, thoroughly enjoying the view of his rear end strutting out of sight.

I didn't say it, but I knew he would not be up for much after his father's funeral. It seemed like all of the wonderful moments spent in our own little world ended with us crashing back down to reality on Earth. I glanced at the clock, and rolled out of bed.

Twenty minutes later, we met the rest of the Brooks family members outside. Beverly had opted to forgo the limousine, so we were waiting to pile into her crossover while she locked up the house.

"Where's your tie?" Chase questioned Tanner.

"He couldn't figure out how to tie it right," Khloe answered quietly.

"So you're just never going to wear a tie because dad's not here to do it for you?"

Tanner ignored him, looking off into the distance.

"You couldn't YouTube it or something?" Chase clearly was not letting this go.

"I did, asshole! Why don't you get the fuck off my back?" Tanner fired back.

"You need to look presentable today!" I had never heard Chase yell before.

"Why? Dad's not here to see me. What the fuck does it matter?"

"Hey! Stop this right now!" Beverly raised her voice at her sons as she scurried down the driveway towards them. "I will have none of that today, do you hear me?"

They both put their heads down. I took Khloe's hand and started walking towards Beverly's car. The ride to the service was quiet after that. Tanner sat in the front with Beverly, silently staring out the window. Even Khloe did not have any questions to ask. The service was being held at a local park. Since Tim's remains were cremated, there would be no headstone at a cemetery. Guests were invited to gather today to remember his life, and the family would take his ashes home when it was over. It made me think about how I had not been to my dad's burial site; I wondered if he minded. I always thought it was such a creepy place, filled with dead bodies buried into holes in the ground. People went there, pretending to communicate with their loved ones – but their loved ones didn't hear them; it was only a comfort for the people who were left behind.

Once we arrived, I sat and observed. I watched as Chase held my hand like it was a life preserver keeping him afloat. I watched Tanner's expressionless face, as if he was carved out of stone. I watched as Khloe sat with her tiny hands folded in her lap, like she was in school; her dark dress was such a contrast against her golden locks. I watched as Beverly kept her composure, only dabbing her eyes at the very end. I watched people kiss their fingers and touch the urn before they left, many of whom were Tim's friends and customers from the shop, to say their final goodbyes.

Shelly and Brody were among the last to leave.

"Thanks for coming, guys," Chase said as he stood to shake Brody's hand. His hand returned to mine as soon as he retracted it.

"Of course," Shelly replied, giving him a squeeze. "I'll never forget him, or what he did for my friend."

I hugged her tightly. "Miss you, Toad."

"Miss you, too, Frog. Call me tomorrow."

I nodded.

Khloe tugged on Beverly's dress. "Mommy? Can I hold daddy in the car?"

"Sure, honey. Just hold it very carefully."

Khloe nodded solemnly. "I will."

And she did. She held the urn in her tiny hands, patting it lovingly every once in a while.

I quickly swiped away a tear that had escaped before anybody saw.

Beverly did not choose to have people back at the house. I completely understood, and was actually relieved that it would be just us.

Tanner went straight to his room, and closed the door.

Beverly made two cups of tea, and set them down on the dining room table.

"Thank you," I said as she slid the cup over to me. I snuck another look at Khloe, who was sitting next to me with the urn in her lap.

"Merry, where are your dad's ashes? Do you have them?"

"No. My dad is in a cemetery."

"That's the place where they put you in the dirt?"

I nodded. "Yep."

Her nose scrunched up in disgust. "Yuck. I would never want to be put in the dirt with all the bugs."

"Me neither."

Chase raised his eyebrows. "Really?"

"The whole idea of being put in a box and buried under the ground is so…" I looked at Khloe and chose my words wisely. "Weird."

Khloe nodded her head feverishly. "So weird!"

Beverly smiled. "I like the idea of having dad here with us."

The tiniest Brooks child hugged the urn. "Me, too."

"Have you visited your dad yet?" Chase asked.

I shook my head, and looked down at my lap. "No. I feel like he would understand. It's not really him that I'd be visiting."

"You don't have to visit a cemetery to remember your father," Beverly offered.

"Do you think about your dad every day?" Khloe innocently asked.

"I do," I replied. "We had a lot of fun times when I was your age."

"Can you tell me a story?"

"It's time for your bath," Beverly intercepted. "You can listen to stories another time. Say goodnight to Chase and Merritt."

"Goodnight?!" She protested. "But it's so early!"

"They're going back to Merritt's place now. You and I can watch a movie after your bath. How does that sound?"

"Can we watch Moana?"

Beverly smiled. "Of course."

I hugged the tiny human.

"I love you, Merry."

I held her face in between my hands. "I love you more!"

She giggled as I squished her cheeks around.

As we walked outside, Tanner followed behind us.

"Where are you off to?" Chase asked.

"Don't you worry about where I'm going." Tanner did not turn around when he spoke.

I put my hand up in front of Chase, to stop him from saying anything else. I pushed him towards the stairs to my apartment. "Just leave him alone."

"Why do you always defend him?" Chase asked once we were inside my apartment.

"Why are you always riding him?" I countered.

"I don't ride him." He ran his fingers through his hair. "He acts like such an asshole."

I nodded. "He does, sometimes. But sometimes you make it worse. Just let him do his thing."

"You really think I ride him?"

"I do. But I know it's only because you care. He doesn't get that."

"But you do." He drew me close to him, playing with a strand of my hair with his fingers. "You always get me."

I didn't have to stretch up so far with my boots on. I met his lips with mine and hugged him as tightly as I could. "I will always get you. Even if I don't, I'll always try to."

"I'm so glad I had you with me today."

"I'm glad I was able to be there."

"I can't imagine you not being around."

"You don't have to imagine that. I'm here."

He sighed. "You don't know what it was like that night. You don't remember much. But I remember every detail."

"The night of my accident?"

"Yeah." He took my hands and led me to the couch to sit. "I was following behind you, and you were all over the road. I tried to pull up next to you, but you almost sideswiped me. Then, you took off. You were going so fast, and I had to go faster just to keep up with you. I don't know what happened but all of a sudden your car just veered to the right… you hit that tree so hard. I ran out of my car – I barely put it in park. There was glass everywhere. You were sitting there with your eyes closed, blood streaming down your face." His eyes began to fill with tears. "I thought you were dead. When I tugged on your arm and realized that you were stuck, you opened your eyes. The flames had started, and smoke was filling the car, so I called my dad. He told me to stay away from the car, in case it blew up. But I couldn't. I couldn't leave you in there by yourself. You were coughing, and your eyes looked terrified. I tried to pull you out, but no matter what I did, I couldn't get you out of there."

I stroked his cheek with my thumb. "But you did get me out of there. You called for help and everything is fine now. I'm here. I'm okay, and I'll never do something like that again."

"Sometimes, before I fall asleep at night, I can see you stuck inside your car. It scares the shit out of me."

I nodded. "My dreams were pretty scary, too. But it's all over. We don't have to think about that anymore. We need to focus on the present, and our future."

He smiled. "Our future?"

"Yes. Eyes ahead, focused on where we're going. Not where we've been."

"And where do you see our future going?"

"What do I look like, a fortune teller?"

"Oh, you're funny now?" He flipped me onto my back on the couch, tickling me relentlessly while I squirmed underneath him.

I squealed with laughter. "I've… always… been funny," I gasped in between giggles.

It felt good, yet strange to laugh. The relentless storm had finally passed us, and sunlight was streaking through the dark clouds.

We could finally be happy. No strings attached.

Chapter Twenty-two: Full of Surprises

"This weather is so crappy. We should have just ordered in."

Chase sighed. "It's just a little snow. I am not letting my girlfriend order in on her birthday."

I leaned over onto the driver's side and kissed his cheek. "I love it when you call me that."

"What, my girlfriend?"

"Yes."

He grinned. "I know you wouldn't have minded staying in tonight, but I just couldn't do it. Not this time, anyway. We'll have plenty of birthdays to stay in. This birthday is special."

"Why, because of the whole I-almost-died-but-didn't thing?"

"Yes, that… and because it's our first time spending your birthday together. The first of many."

"Fine. But if you think you're always going to win every fight with your adorableness, you need to think again."

"I will ride out these good looks as far as they'll take me."

"They got you this far."

I stared out the window at the old Victorian-style house we were pulling up to. White with black shutters, string lights lit up the wraparound porch. With Valentine's Day only a week away, red hearts decorated every window upstairs and downstairs.

"Aww Chase! I've heard such good things about this place. I've always wanted to try it, but it's a little out of my price range."

"Tonight, you don't need to worry about the price. It's your night. My baby eats whatever she wants."

"Are you sure about that? Your baby is hungry."

He chuckled as he turned into a spot. "It looks packed. Good thing I made reservations."

I loved seeing him in better spirits. He had his good days and his bad days since Tim's passing.

We threw our hoods on when we stepped out of the car, and trudged through the snow as quickly as we could to get out of the whipping wind. Once inside, we shook off our coats. Chase gave his name to the hostess.

"Right this way," she gestured with a smile.

"It's so pretty in here," I whispered to Chase as we followed the hostess up a flight of creaky wooden stairs. Upstairs, the same red and pink hearts in the windows hung from the ceiling. Small tealight candles sat atop each linen-covered table. I was too busy taking in the scenery to notice who was sitting at the table we were brought to.

"Surprise!" everyone yelled.

I jumped, and my hands flew up to my open mouth. Shelly, Brody, Tina, Kenzie, Beverly, Tanner, a girl I slightly recognized, and Khloe stood around the long rectangular table, laughing at my shocked reaction.

"Oh my God!" I turned to Chase and playfully smacked him on the arm.

"Happy birthday, beautiful." He pulled me in and kissed my forehead.

"Well, don't take all the credit!" Shelly scurried around the table and threw her arms around me. "Happy birthday, Merr!"

"You guys are the best. Thank you so much."

I felt a small human clinging to my leg. "Happy birthday, Merry!"

I knelt down to give Khloe a proper hug. "I'm so glad you're at my party!"

"Me too. Mommy said I can stay up later tonight."

"Well, lucky you!" I looked over at Tanner, who had his arm around the new girl's waist. "And who might this be?"

"His new flavor of the week," Chase muttered under his breath.

"This is Charlotte." Tanner introduced us.

I held out my hand. "It's very nice to meet you, Charlotte. You moved here not too long ago, didn't you?"

She nodded shyly. "Yeah, about a year ago."

She was not someone I expected Tanner to bring home. She looked like a sweet, girl-next-door type. She was pretty with blonde hair and blue eyes, but very plain. I was intrigued to see how their dynamic worked. Opposites do attract, after all. I looked up at Chase and wondered if people looked at us in the same way.

I sat in between Chase and Khloe, of course, with Shelly across from me. I looked around the table, amazed at how my circle had grown since meeting Chase. Once everyone had their drinks in hand, I raised my water glass.

"Thank you guys for being here tonight. This surprise means so much to me. I love you all so much."

We all clinked glasses. Khloe made sure to cheers every person at the table with her plastic cup of apple juice.

Halfway through dinner, I noticed Chase periodically checking his phone.

"Everything okay?" I whispered.

"Yeah. I keep getting calls from this number."

"Did they leave a message?"

"No."

"Maybe you should just answer it. Tell them they've got the wrong number."

"If they call back, I will."

I nodded, and didn't think about it any further. The night was filled with funny stories and laughter. After everything we had all gone through, it felt so good to come together under happier circumstances.

After the cake came out, Chase stood up with his phone in hand. "I'm going to take this. I'll be right back."

I nodded as I stabbed my slice of chocolate cake and shoved a huge bite into my mouth.

"Do you like it?" Charlotte asked.

I tried to speak. "It's delicious."

She giggled as the crumbs spilled out of my mouth. "Good. I'm glad. My parents own the new bakery in Woodrow Plaza. That's where we got your cake from."

I wiped my mouth with the napkin, trying to look civilized in front of the newcomer. "Very cool. I'd love to see what else they have there."

Tanner looked happy. His brows were not in their usual furrowed stance; his lips were curled up instead of down. I wanted to ask questions about how the two met, but I did not want to make them awkward. Everyone always gave Tanner a hard time, and I wanted to let him be tonight.

Chase returned to the table after several minutes, shoving his phone back into his pocket.

"Wrong number?" I asked.

He nodded. "Yup. How's the cake?"

"It's so good. Charlotte's family owns a bakery."

"Nice." He took a bite of the cake waiting on his plate. He seemed uncharacteristically quiet for the remainder of the party. Planning a surprise party can be stressful, so I pushed the strange feeling in my gut down and away.

Driving home, though, Chase did not say two words. His gaze was far away as we pulled up to the house, and he killed the engine.

"Are you staying over tonight?" I asked. He had been spent every night at my apartment since Christmas.

"Sure. If you want me to."

I scrunched my face up in confusion. "If I want you to?"

"Yeah, I mean if you're tired we can just call it a night."

"If I'm tired?" I sighed. "Alright. Who's the girl?"

He turned in his seat to look at me. "What?"

"Your phone has been ringing with an unknown caller. You don't seem like yourself. And now you're too tired to give me birthday sex. These are clear signs that you're talking to another girl."

To my surprise, he started laughing.

"And now you're laughing. Cool." I swung open the passenger door.

"Merritt, no." He got out of his car and chased me up the driveway. "Let's go inside and I'll explain everything. There is no other girl."

I stopped just before the stairs. "If you try to give me some bullshit excuse, I'm going to know you're lying… and then I'll have no choice but to chop off your balls."

He held my face with both hands. "You are the only girl I want in my life. I love you. Please let me explain what's really going on… and please don't chop off my balls."

I quickly went to my bedroom to change into comfortable sweats, and swept my hair up in a bun. I sat on the couch, the suspense killing me slowly with every passing second.

Chase sat down on the couch beside me, his phone in hand. "Listen to this voicemail, and then I'll tell you everything."

I suspiciously took his phone from his hands and pushed play:

"Hey, Chase! This is Billy Montgomery, out in California. I got a call from Donnie the other day. He played our demo for an up-and-coming record label out here. They loved it, man. The guys and I were hoping you'd be able to come back. We need a lead singer, and you were the voice he heard on the demo. Hit me back at this number. This is big news, man!"

Silence filled the room after the voicemail ended. I was still, letting the message fully sink in.

"So," Chase began. "Billy is the guitarist in the band I sang with when I was out in California last year."

I nodded.

"I guess they are still using the demo we recorded, with me on the lead vocals."

I nodded, again.

"Donnie is the guy who owned the bar I worked at. He's the one who helped spread our names around town."

I wanted to cry; I knew I couldn't. I couldn't show him that his leaving would hurt me. I was a college dropout who had no clear path ahead of me. I would live a simple life, with a simple job, living in a simple town. I couldn't be the one to hold him back from greatness. He had the talent and the true potential to make something of himself. Who was I to stand in his way? I sat back on the couch and took a deep breath. "That's great news. A new record label would be a great opportunity for you to start with."

Chase's eyes narrowed. "Merritt, I'm not going back to California."

"You're not?"

"No. Of course not. I have you now, and I'm helping my mom and Tanner at the shop. That ship has sailed."

"You came home because your dad was sick. He isn't here anymore. Your mom and Tanner are running the shop just fine. Plus now they have me."

His mouth nearly dropped into his lap. "And what about us?"

I shrugged. "I'd still be here. This is your dream we're talking about."

"So, you're telling me you think I should go to California and start a whole new life."

"No. I'm telling you to go to California and live your dream. It would be a new chapter in your same old life."

He ran his fingers through his hair. "I can't believe you're saying this right now."

"I can't believe you're saying you won't go."

"I didn't think it was even an option." He looked down at his hands in his lap. "I thought you'd want me to stay."

I raised his chin up so he would look me in the eye. "I always want to be with you. I don't want you to leave me. I want you to be happy."

"I am happy when I'm with you."

"Then don't screw some California groupie chick, and you'll have me."

"I meant what I said before. I don't want anybody else. You're it for me."

"Good. Then pursuing your dreams on the other side of the country won't change anything between us. I'll be here waiting for you when you come back."

"Come with me."

I laughed. "Yeah. Right."

"Why not? You don't have anything tying you to this place."

"I couldn't just leave Tanner by himself to work in the shop."

"My mom was talking about selling the place."

"Yeah, if they couldn't keep the business afloat. I can help them keep it afloat. They would be crushed to lose your dad's shop. Wouldn't you?"

Chase shrugged. "It was never my thing. I always had other plans for my future. If they can't make it work, they should just sell it and be done with all the stress."

I played with the strings from my hood. "I couldn't move to California. You'd be busy, but what would I do?"

"Why not go to school there? Finish getting your Bachelor's Degree, and go from there. We can get an apartment together. I can bartend for cash."

"You really put a lot of thought into this plan, huh?"

He slid his wallet out of his back pocket. He flicked through his money inside, and took out two white pieces of paper. "I was actually banking on it."

In his outstretched hand were two airline tickets – one of which had my name on it.

"Chase…" I began.

"Please don't say no right away," he begged. "If you don't want to come with me, then I'm not going anywhere. It's both of us, or neither of us."

"No pressure or anything."

"I'm not trying to pressure you. I just need you to see that I want my future to include you, and that I don't want to leave you behind while I go off and fulfill some pipe dream. I know you would love California. After everything we've been through – after everything you've been through – we could get a fresh start, together. If you think about it, and decide that you don't want to go – I can always get a refund for my tickets. Just please don't answer right now. Sleep on it."

I flopped backward onto the couch, staring up at the ceiling.

Sleep on it. As if I'd actually get any sleep after this.

Chapter Twenty-three: The Knock

"He wants you to move where?!"

I winced in pain. "I think you scrambled my brain with that octave."

"There is no way you are considering actually going with him, are you?"

I uncovered my ears. "Is it safe to come out?"

"Be serious, Merr. What are the odds that he's going to be the next big star? And what are you going to do while he's off playing gigs in bars? You'll be all alone."

"He brought up going to school there."

"How are you going to afford all the expenses? California isn't cheap."

"I know. It all sounds crazy."

"That's because it is crazy."

Brody sighed loudly.

"Oh, don't you dare say a word right now," Shelly warned.

Brody smiled. "Listen, I know you two are best friends, and you don't want to be apart from each other. But she's my best friend, too, and I have to be honest with her. What else are they going to do stuck here for the rest of their lives?"

"I cannot believe I'm hearing this." Shelly covered her face with her hands.

"Dude, you should have just agreed with her." I winked at Brody.

"She knows I'm right." He rubbed her knee. "You can't stop her from going any more than she can stop Chase from going. It just wouldn't be right."

"I haven't made my decision, yet. I'm just bouncing it off of you."

"Who would you bounce it off of in California, huh?" Shelly fired. "You'd be out there all by yourself."

"She could use this nifty new invention called a phone," Brody retorted.

"No! You're not on my side. You don't get to use sarcasm."

I stifled a laugh. Shelly actually looked like she was genuinely upset.

"This is crazy." She shook her head. "What about the shop? What will Tanner and Beverly do without you? What about Khloe? She would be heartbroken with you."

"Geeze, Shell. Don't use the kid to guilt her into staying."

I nodded. "She's right. These are the things I brought up to Chase last night."

"What did he say to that?" she asked, with hope in her eyes.

"He said that his mom might be selling the place."

Brody's eyebrows lifted. "Really? That's surprising."

"That's Tim's shop – how could they sell it?"

"I don't know their finances or anything, but I don't know how they can manage with Tim gone. I told Chase to go without me, and that I would help his mom and Tanner in the shop. Maybe we could hire an extra person so the workload wouldn't be too much."

Shelly's eyes widened as if I had just told her I had one day left to live. "Merritt, no! You cannot let him go without you. That's the kiss of death!"

Brody shook his head. "Don't listen to her."

"I'm serious. You've seen how girls act around Chase. California would be like high school all over again; only this time, the girls would have fake boobs and modeling contracts."

I grimaced at the thought.

"Don't go putting these crazy thoughts in her head." Brody leaned towards me. "Chase loves you, Merr. He's crazy about you, and everyone knows it."

"All he has to do is tell those twits about the time he saved someone from a burning car." Shelly shook her head. "They'll be dropping their panties like it is Spring Break at Cabo."

"You're like a demonic Jiminy Cricket, you know that?" I laughed it off, but I wanted to vomit at the thought of Chase and panty-dropping models.

She shrugged. "It's my job as your best friend to keep it real."

"Keeping it real would mean you help her weigh the pros and cons of a major decision like this – not scare her into making the decision you want her to make."

Brody was right. Shelly knew it, and I knew it.

A knock at my door signaled Chase had arrived. Shelly was closest to the door, so she got up to open it. She rolled her eyes when she saw who it was. "Why are you even knocking?"

He walked in, his eyebrows raised. "Hello to you, too."

Brody laughed, shaking his head. "Watch out, man. Your biggest fan has turned into your worst nightmare."

Chase flopped onto the couch, leaning over to give me a kiss. "Uh-oh. I'm guessing you told her."

"Yes. Apparently, going to California with you is a terrible idea; but if I don't go, you'll be cheating on me with panty-dropping models." I used air quotes to emphasize the model part.

Now Brody was not the only one in the room shaking his head. "You really think that I would do something like that, Shell?"

Her arms were crossed over her chest. "You're Chase Brooks."

He almost choked as he laughed. "You've got to be kidding me! You're the one who was pushing us together this whole time, and now I'm back to being that Chase Brooks?"

Shelly stood, frustrated, with her little girly hands clenched into fists. "I almost lost my best friend in a horrific car accident, and now you want to move her across the entire country? Do you have no heart?!"

Chase sat up, a soft, sincere expression on his face. "I told her: if she doesn't want to go together, then I don't want to go at all. Her happiness means everything to me."

"Well, she's very happy here with her best friend," Shelly replied matter-of-factly.

I giggled at how difficult she was being. "And I told him that his happiness means everything to me, too. I would never hold him back from doing something he wanted to do… unless it involves panty-dropping." I shot him the death stare for good measure. "Think about it. If you knew Brody's dream was to do something, you would never want to be the one to stand in his way. That's the kind of shit that builds resentment."

Brody nodded silently.

"Does that mean you're considering coming with me?" Chase asked in a quiet voice.

"I'm considering the pros and cons of each option."

"That's better than a straight up no," Brody offered. He stood, tossing his jacket over his shoulder. "Come on, babe. Let's give these two some time to discuss everything."

She stood in a huff, thrusting her arms angrily into her jacket. "Fine. But once you decide you're running off to California, don't decide that you're leaving immediately. You have to give me fair warning."

"What's fair?" Chase asked, curious.

"At least a week!"

I covered my ears. "Not again! My ears were just recovering."

She made a face at me, and swung the door open.

Brody took my hand, pulling me off the couch to hug me. "Make the best decision for you. Not Shelly, and not Chase. You deserve to be happy, so follow your happiness. Do you hear me?"

I nodded, wrapping my arms tightly around his midsection. "I would miss you, too, you know."

His cheeks pushed up into his Cheshire cat grin. "Ditto, Adams. You were my very first friend here. Don't forget about me."

I waved goodbye as they trotted down the stairs, and closed the door behind them.

Chase heaved a loud sigh. "Think Shelly will ever forgive me if I take you away?"

"I'm not sure. That girl knows how to hold a grudge."

"So… which way are you leaning towards?"

I laid my head in his lap, hanging my legs over the arm of the couch. "I keep imagining myself standing at a fork in the road. I have two paths ahead of me, and either way I get to be with you."

Chase twirled a lock of my curls around his finger, listening quietly.

"If I go down one path, you will get to have the experience of a lifetime, and fulfill your true potential. I will get to watch you make your dreams come true. In turn, that will fill me with so much joy. This path, however, is absolutely terrifying for me. I'd be moving to a place where I know nothing, and no one. I can't see my future down this path."

"And the other path?"

"The other path, I can see my future very clearly. We would work at the shop, and stay close to your family and my friends. We'd get to watch Khloe grow up before our eyes. Your mom wouldn't be so lonely. I know I'd be happy, because I'm already happy now with the way things are going for us."

"But?"

"But… there would always be that nagging feeling in my gut. The kind of feeling that wakes you from a dead sleep ten years down the line, when you ask yourself if your life could have been more. I don't want to have that feeling, and worse, I don't want you to have it."

Chase nodded as he ran his fingers through his hair. "Those are the same questions I have racing around in my mind."

"Want to know what I keep thinking about? That Robert Frost poem."

A smile crept onto his face. "The one about the road less traveled?"

"Yup. That terrifying untraveled road."

"You did say you wanted to live life to the fullest."

Just then, a knock came at my door.

"How much you want to bet this is Shelly?" I jumped up and ran to the door.

"Tears running down her face, sobbing about how horrible your boyfriend is for taking you away from her," Chase chimed in.

I swung the door open, and my heart almost stopped beating on the spot. I was frozen where I stood, unable to move or make a sound. It was as if all of the air had been sucked out of the room as I struggled to take a breath of air.

"Who is it?" Chase's voice sounded muffled by the sound of the blood pounding in my ears.

"Hi, Merritt."

Chase was now standing by my side, peering out from behind the doorframe. His stunned expression matched mine.

"It's…" I couldn't get the words out. "It's my mom."

THE END

Dear Reader,

Something about this book has made you decide to buy it. Maybe it was the cover that intrigued you; maybe it was the blurb I wrote to summarize the story; maybe a friend read it, and recommended it to you. Whatever the reason was – thank you.

I have gone through major life changes while writing this book. I have been through marriage, divorce, remarriage, and became a step-mother, all while writing this story – and I'm only in my thirties! It is a story that has been in my head for quite some time now, and I am still in utter disbelief that it has come to this point – the point where you are reading these words.

Buying a book, however cheap it may be, requires a certain level of trust. One reads the summary, and decides that the author and story seem worthy of his or her time and money. I hope that I don't disappoint you. If you enjoyed it, won't you please take a moment to leave me a review at your favorite retailer? Thank You!

Kristen

Follow me on Instagram:
https://www.instagram.com/kristen_granata/

Follow me on Facebook:
https://www.facebook.com/kristen.granata.16

Visit my website: https://kristengranata.com/

Printed in Great Britain
by Amazon

81120234R00132